A Force of Habit

A Sister Abigail Mystery

A Force of Habit

SHAROLD SHAW PUBLISHERS

Wheaton, Illinois

This is a work of fiction. The incidents, characters, and setting of this book are products of the author's imagination.

ISBN 0-87788-261-4
Cover illustration by Margaret Sykora
Cover and interior design by Thomas Leo
Typesetting by Carol Barnstable

07 06 05 04 03 02 01 00
10 9 8 7 6 5 4 3 2 1

To my editor, Lil Copan, who opened the door.
And to the One who gives my life joy, purpose,
and meaning.

The Tranquil Garden Community

The Staff

Mother Francesca
Nursing Home Director
Sisters of Mercy
Perpetual vows: May 15, 1949

Sister Angelica
Second Floor Supervisor
Sisters of Mercy
May 22, 1998

Sister Janice
Asst. to the Director
Sisters of Mercy
May 22, 1998

Sister Josephine
Daily Operations
Sisters of Mercy
May 19, 1972

Sister Judith
First Floor Supervisor
Sisters of Mercy
May 22, 1998

Robert Forrester
Lay volunteer

Tom Wallins
Janitor

The Residents

Sister Abigail
Contemplative
Sisters of the Divine Name
May 2, 1926

Sister Clare
Hospice Nurse (retired)
Sisters of the Sacred Heart
June 3, 1948

Sister Graciella
Missionary
Sisters of the Incarnate Word
July 21, 1933

Sister Gloria
Nurse (retired)
Sisters of the Sacred Heart
June 5, 1929

Sister Kathlee
High School Principal (retired)
Community of the Holy Family
June 7, 1935

Sister Monica
Schoolteacher (retired)
Sisters of Loretto
May 19, 1939

Sister Patrice
Nurse (retired)
Sisters of the Precious Blood
June 8, 1937

Sister Florence
Nurse (retired)
Sisters of the Sacred Heart
June 18, 1939

The Visitors

Sister Emily
Administrator (retired)
Daughters of Charity
April 30, 1948

Sister Alicia
Contemplative
Sisters of the Divine Name
June 4, 1994

Tranquil Garden Nursing Home
First Floor

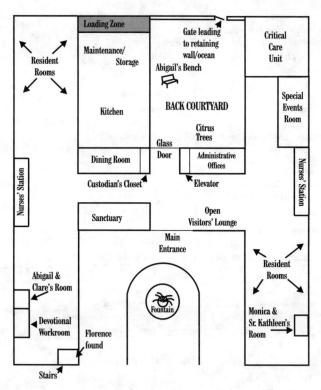

S
E —|— W
N

Loading Zone

Resident Rooms

Maintenance/ Storage

Gate leading to retaining wall/ocean

Critical Care Unit

Abigail's Bench

Kitchen

BACK COURTYARD

Special Events Room

Citrus Trees

Glass Door

Dining Room

Administrative Offices

Nurses' Station

Custodian's Closet

Elevator

Sanctuary

Open Visitors' Lounge

Main Entrance

Nurses' Station

Resident Rooms

Abigail & Clare's Room

Devotional Workroom

Fountain

Monica & Sr. Kathleen's Room

Florence found

Stairs

Prologue

Deathwatch: Sisters of the Divine Name Mother-house, Westbury, Massachusetts

Hour by hour I watch the light from the vigil candles dance on the white plaster walls. Death approaches slowly.

The cause of my bodily demise is not old age, although I am advanced in years. It is not by natural causes that I leave this life. I am being murdered.

It began with an unusual taste in my afternoon tea. Dose by dose the poison progresses in completing the evil act. Soon it will be over without anyone realizing the vicious deed. I will say nothing. If it were to be otherwise, He would have made it so.

As death nears so does new life. The relief from the suffering will be welcomed, as will the One that I have longed to see for as many years as I have known breath.

What a sacred honor it is to be dying within the confines of this convent. From my first step past the heavy wooden door that shuts out the rest of the world, I have felt unworthy to walk its halls. But here is where the Lord would have me stay for more than seventy years.

My years of service began with hours of study on the first floor, the same way they began for so many Sisters before me. And, just like the others, my years will end in this room. The room where death meets life.

I remember my early days in this consecrated house. Autumn's leaves in their varying shades of golden red thickly covered the ground like snow. Winter's gray skies, and that endless cold; it seemed my feet would never be warm again. But spring finally came, filling the air with its fragrance. It was then that I was summoned into the fellowship called The Order; twelve sisters called by God to live a calling within a calling.

The ways of God are many, and those within The Order strove to be open to every possibility. I was entrusted with the gift of prophetic visions. Some of those visions saw fulfillment during the years of my life; others will come to pass after my death. But one vision will be lived out in this room before I breathe my last. In those last moments, I pass on the mantle of graces set aside for the one anointed who will take my place among the twelve. And it will be soon.

What music the Sisters' prayers are to my ears. What a delight their voices are to me. I can not separate their voices. None are higher.

None are lower. It is as if there is only one voice. They come each morning, escorting me with their prayers as the final days of this journey pass.

Will I miss the smells of earth? These freshly laundered linens, the smoldering wick of a candle, and . . . it couldn't be. Yes, there is no mistaking the delightful fragrance, the same one that accompanied the prophetic vision concerning The Order. It was granted to me one summer night less than a year ago. The Spirit of the Lord came upon me without warning. Gently. Lovingly. He delivered His message with simple clarity. I thought nothing more of it until now, smelling it afresh. She is here. The anointed one is in the room among the others. The time for me to pass the mantle of graces draws near.

Such innocence I see in her, such purity of heart. Does she know of the evil entering this house? Does she know to what lengths it may go to destroy The Order? Will she understand that even though fierce and wicked, it can not snatch away what is His? No, regardless of how much territory it appears the darkness has gained, in the end, evil will not triumph.

All that is left is to wait. The moment can not be hurried or delayed. It will be in the perfect time of Him who created the seasons and the months of the year. I am certain it will be soon.

The beautiful voices of the novices have said the last Amen. They will go about the tasks of the living while I remain waiting. I feel warmth as a young novice touches my hand, and another kisses my cheek. I hear their blessings as they pass my bedside, strengthening me for my final task: the moment when the ancient question will pass these lips, and the sacred prayer will carry through to the soul of God's anointed, as it carried to mine, as it carried to all those appointed into The Order throughout the centuries of our history.

Now one by one they leave. I am left in silence.

Has an hour passed? A day? It is not for me to know, neither is it for me to know when I will mercifully draw my last breath.

What is that? Approaching footsteps. It is the sound of angel trumpets to my impatient ears, my waiting soul. My final task is now at hand.

Who kneels before me now with head bowed so low that I can not make out an identity? It is not for me to know.

The room grows cold. My bones quiver as the chill of the unholy presence tries to cast its shadow on this Divine event. And yet I smell the Divine fragrance that accompanies the prophetic vision. No, it is not for me to question. If the one before me answers the question correctly, the mantle of graces will pass on—the pleasant odor gives me comfort that it will be so—despite this last battle against darkness.

"Propose me a question before you are drawn from this life."

"First, tell me the vision the Lord has blessed you with."

"He has shown me a white rose in the bloom of spring."

"And how many thorns have sprouted from the stem of this lovely flower?"

"Seven, one for each of the seven deadly sins that can pierce the soul of man."

"Place your hands on me, daughter, and prepare your soul for the gift to come."

"I welcome His gifts."

"By the power of the Divine Name of Jesus Christ, receive the mantle of surrender to this His holy will and the gentle yoke of servanthood to this, His Order."

"I do receive."

My service is complete. Once again I am left to wait. The moment of my death draws near. How sweet it will be.

Fifty-four years later

The Gulf of Mexico sent small waves gliding up the sandy Texas shore with the same rhythmic constancy it has known for thousands of years. A January morning approached, but there was still no hint of the coming light at the horizon. A retaining wall, built decades earlier to slow beach erosion, stood with silent brawn a short distance from the furthest reaches of the boldest waves, and beyond that stood the massive two-story complex known as the Tranquil Garden Nursing Home.

Run by the Sisters of Mercy, the home had been purchased for the sole purpose of housing women who had lived the consecrated life of a religious. Many of the residents were themselves Sisters of Mercy: a society dedicated to ensuring consolation and comfort in the final years of nuns' lives.

The two-story colonial Spanish structure, with its arched doorways and red roof tiles, was made up of two lengthy wings running north and south. An east/west hallway joined the wings at the center. The result, a formidable architecture of the letter *H*—an impressive sight, even at a distance.

The clock near the center of the main floor's east/west hallway read a quarter after five, and the door to the custodian's closet beneath it stood open. Further down the hall a short man with a protruding middle pushed a cart and a rolling mop bucket into position. Tom Wallins was about to begin his workday.

His work progressed as the sun lazily rose above the horizon. As he reached for his broom a cold chill ran over him. He turned as if expecting to see something. He looked first to the left, then to the right, but nothing was there.

Beads of sweat formed on his brow. His breath came in short, shallow spurts. It was not the first time he had felt this presence within the walls of Tranquil Garden, but recently it had begun to press about him with a new intensity.

He suddenly felt a cold metal object touch along the back of his sweat-soaked shirt. His face paled. As he turned, he discovered he had backed into an open door.

"You scared me half out of my skin, Sister Abigail."

An elderly woman wearing thick glasses made her way through the opened door. "Good morning, Tom."

"Isn't it early for you to be visiting in the Critical Care Unit?"

"They brought Sister Agnes in about an hour ago."

"I'm sorry to hear that. She just got out of there yesterday morning."

"You're out of breath."

"The bump from the door gave me more of a start than I thought." He leaned against his broom. "That's been going on too much lately. I don't like jumping at the sight of my own shadow around here."

"And you aren't the only one who is," she whispered. She began making her way past the janitor's cart. "But do not fear," she said in a louder voice, "the darkness that has descended on this place has chosen to dwell among those who constantly invoke the name of Jesus. Rest assured, it will no doubt exhaust itself from all its constant shuddering."

The old woman faltered slightly.

"Let me get you to the railing, Sister." He reached for her hand. "I hear today is a special day for you."

"My new roommate is arriving."

"It will be nice for you to have some company."

"If we are compatible, I agree; otherwise

the experience will seem more like lengthy penance."

He let go of her hand. "You let me know if she's not."

Abigail smiled. "I intend to let everyone know."

Tom watched until the nun safely turned the corner before he returned his broom to its rightful spot and began making his way toward the nursing home entrance. He stepped outside and sniffed the morning sea air as he searched the front pocket of his blue coveralls. He approached a gangly looking young man who was sitting on a bench.

"Morning," Tom said.

The man looked up. "Morning."

"Mind if I sit?"

"Help yourself."

Tom sat down and put the stub of a cigar into his mouth. "They won't let me smoke inside."

"They don't let you smoke anywhere nowadays."

Tom studied the man's uniform. "Did you deliver something?"

"Medical supplies. What kind of place is this?"

"It's a nursing home for nuns."

"They told me to wait inside, but the place kinda gives me the shakes. If I need to wait that's fine, but I'll do it out here." The man pulled a cigarette from his pocket. "They have that many old nuns?"

"They come from all over the country when they get too old to do their work." Tom shook his head. "They never had children, so visitors are few. They all left places they spent their whole lives. They come here where they don't know anybody. It's sad if you ask me."

The man drew on his cigarette. "Who's that coming up the driveway?"

"Sister Janice. The Sisters of Mercy have a handful of young ones. See that building further down over there? The nuns from that convent run this nursing home."

"She doesn't look like a nun."

"Their convent stopped wearing habits before that one was ever born." Tom motioned to the man's cigarette. "Better put that out."

"Why?"

"She'll give you a hard time if you don't."

Sister Janice smiled warmly. "Good morning, Tom."

"It's a better one now, Sister."

"And who is your friend?"

"I'm William. I mean Will." He got to his feet quickly and unfolded a yellow piece of paper. "I have an invoice for you to sign."

The young woman looked into his eyes until he nervously looked away. "I'll need a pen."

"Here," he said, as he pulled a pen from his pocket and removed the cap.

She signed the paper and handed it back, then stood quietly until he walked off. "I thought you weren't going to have any more cigars, Tom."

"This one's different," he answered. "Sister Helen asked her nephew to send me one of these and it finally came yesterday." He bent over and snuffed it out on the concrete. "Turning the cigar down would be like turning her down."

"She is very sensitive about that kind of thing, but smoking cigars will do vile things to your mouth and throat."

"Yes, Sister. I'm through with them for good this time."

She walked away, then quickened her step at the sight of a woman standing near the front entrance. "Good morning, Mother Francesca."

"There still is no word on our new arrivals."

Sister Janice followed her superior into the building. "The itinerary called for the new residents to fly into Houston yesterday evening and spend the night at the Sacred Heart convent."

"It was my understanding they were to arrive by van first thing this morning."

The women stopped at a desk near the rear of the visitors' lounge.

Sister Janice sat down and opened an address book. "I'll call and verify their time of arrival."

"Are those our new residents' files?"

"The top three."

Mother Francesca grasped the folders with her aged hands and closed her eyes as if praying a silent, secret blessing. "They have each been assigned separate rooms?"

"As you requested."

Her eyes opened. "Good. I will remember your efficiency when it comes time to consider the administrative position Sister Marie holds." Sister Janice smiled and straightened her posture as she returned the files. Mother Francesca continued: "We will speak about this again."

"Yes, Mother."

A beam of sunlight bouncing off the metal bumper of a gray van shone through the window and caught Mother Francesca's attention. "I see your phone call will not be necessary," she said as she looked out. "Our new residents are here."

"I'll tell the other Sisters to come."

After walking out the main entrance, Mother Francesca stood by the side of a large van as other Sisters of Mercy arrived to help. Each nun went about her duties silently, reverently. In a short time, the three new residents were assembled in the visitors' lounge.

Standing in front of the small group, she said, "I am Mother Francesca. Welcome to the Tranquil Garden Nursing Home. This property was given to the Sisters of Mercy for the sole purpose of providing a resting place, a Nazareth, for you, the brides of Christ. I thank you for allowing us, the least of His children, to serve your needs. You must be tired after your journey, but perhaps you'd like for me to answer some of your questions."

Sister Gloria raised her hand. "Are our rooms close by?"

"You are Sister Gloria, I presume? You and Sister Florence will be on the second floor. And Sister Clare's room is on the first floor."

"I thought—" Sister Florence began.

"Yes?" Mother Francesca waited.

"It was nothing."

There was a silence.

Finally Sister Gloria spoke up. "I think what Sister Florence wanted to say is that she and I have always shared a room. And since all three of us are from the same convent, we were hoping to stay together."

Sister Janice stepped forward. "And you will be for meals, and during any of the recreational hours in your daily schedule." She glanced at Mother Francesca. "May I show them the dining room?"

"Excellent idea. I will leave our new residents in your care."

Sister Janice signaled to another nun. "Let's find a wheelchair for Sister Clare."

"I prefer to walk."

"After your rigorous journey, I think not." She nodded as the nun returned with the chair. "Now, let's be on our way."

The entourage moved down the east/west hallway and into the dining room.

"There is no assigned seating," Sister Janice said, "but the tables without chairs are for the non-ambulatory residents. You will find that the food is delicious here and almost always made from scratch." She waited a moment. "Across the hall is the sanctuary." She began walking again. "This way."

As they entered, they saw the sun filter in through several arched windows and bounce brightly off the finely polished tile floor. The room smelled of freshly cut flowers, which were gathered into baskets on either side of the linen-covered altar. The group went up the center aisle to an area on the left that had no pews.

The sanctuary fell silent after a final squeak from one of the wheelchairs. "Father Joseph celebrates Mass on Tuesday, Thursday, and Sunday mornings, and confessions are heard prior to Mass on Thursday." Sister Janice motioned to the other Sisters of Mercy. "I think a few moments of privacy would be beneficial to our new residents." She patted Sister Florence's shoulder gently. "We will return shortly."

The sound of fading footsteps echoed briefly.

Instead of silently meditating, Florence turned to look at Gloria and Clare. Fear filled her eyes. "I . . . I don't know what it is, but I don't want to stay here."

"*Want* is not a word for us to use," said Gloria.

"But there is something in this place. Something that is not of God."

"I know," Gloria said somberly. "It invades this whole building. Someone here is choosing to walk with the powers of darkness."

Florence gripped the armrest of her wheelchair. "I won't stay here," she said with growing desperation. "I have to get away from this place."

"But you can't leave," Gloria said.

"We could go back to the convent."

"No, Florence," Clare said. "This is our home now. There is nowhere else for us to go."

"I don't think I can stand it," Florence said. "Not alone. To be separated from both of you . . . it's too heavy a burden!"

"Shhh. Keep your voice down," Gloria warned. "You must not fall into a panic."

Florence turned her head toward Clare. "Do you feel it?"

"Yes, very strongly." Sister Clare lifted her hand and placed it over Florence's. "But we should remember that He is ever faithful."

"But—" Sister Florence began.

Sister Gloria nodded her head. "Clare is

right. We have no means of leaving this place, and nowhere to go if we could leave. We must stay and trust. Regardless of whatever harm comes to these worn-out bodies of ours, our eternal souls will be preserved."

Florence turned to Clare. "I can't go back out there, I can't. You and Gloria are strong in faith," she said with a shaking voice. "I am weak. If I am put to the test, I will fail."

"His faithfulness does not rely on our strength," Clare said as she gave Florence's hand a gentle squeeze. "Be at peace. He is ever faithful."

Two

Awakening from her nap, Clare opened her eyes to a stream of sunlight bursting through a gap in the curtains. She wanted to continue facing the light, but an ache in her right shoulder caused her to turn away from the mesmerizing sight.

"Look who is finally stirring about! I thought you might sleep the entire day. You must have traveled a great distance to be so tired."

Clare saw a nun wearing a full habit sitting on the other bed. Her wrinkled face encompassed dim eyes covered by oversized glasses.

"Good day to you," Clare said.

"I was beginning to think you would never wake! My name is Sister Abigail. I am your roommate."

"I'm Sister Clare," she said as she sat up. "What time is it?"

"We have a clock on our wall, but I must confess I can't read it. Did you know you were on my bed?"

"Forgive me, Sister, I didn't know."

"Please, just call me Abigail and I will call you Clare, and all that energy we save from dropping the *Sister,* will give us a few extra days to serve Our Lord."

"Then, Abigail, let me return this bed to your care."

"Stay where you are. That will be your bed, and this one will be mine."

"Are you sure?"

"It will not be a great transition. I will simply take my rosary from this bedpost," she said as she reached for the black beaded rosary. "And place it on this bedpost. There, I am all moved in." Abigail sat down again. "You somehow seem familiar. My eyes have little usefulness these days—with the exception of an occasional blurred glimpse of that wonderful shoreline out there. What do you look like?"

"I don't know," Clare answered. "I'm old."

"Of course you are!" Abigail cackled with laughter. "Yes, I think compatible will describe us. What convent are you from?"

"The Sisters of the Sacred Heart."

"And what was your work?"

"I sat."

"Indeed. Is that all you did?"

"I was a companion for the dying."

Abigail nodded. "Admirable work." Then she asked, "Do you make rosaries?"

"It's been years."

"Then you must join us today and meet some of the other Sisters." She adjusted her glasses. "Our table holds six, but we have been five due to the failing health of Sister Agnes. Your labors would be a blessing."

"Then I gladly offer them."

"We drop the *Sister* from all names except Sister Kathleen's. We are in the practice of saving the formal address for when our memory has failed us, but she can grow quite testy if addressed in a common fashion. She spent many years as the principal of a high school, and takes discipline and respect very seriously. Now, Patrice is quite the opposite, having an attitude that almost nothing needs to be taken seriously. As you can imagine, they are often in conflict."

Clare waited for Abigail to continue. "You said there were five."

"Five what?"

"In your group that makes rosaries."

"Oh, yes. I didn't tell you about Monica or Graciella. Both are of a more quiet nature. Monica is like a crystal figurine: on the delicate side. Tears come to her easily and frequently. And Graciella was a missionary who was out of the country so long she had to relearn English." Abigail leaned forward. "We've known each other. I'm sure of it."

"I don't think so."

"Did you ever attend a retreat at St. Benedict's?"

"No."

"It's a breathtaking place. When I am finished here, I am scheduled for four glorious days within its ivy-covered walls."

"You will leave Tranquil Garden?"

"I am only here for the winter. When spring arrives I will return to the Motherhouse of my community. I believe this year I am the only temporary resident at Tranquil Garden. Last year there were several of us and we gathered frequently in the back courtyard to smell the intoxicating citrus trees and reminisce about our years of service." When she heard sounds outside the door, Abigail stood up. "My eyes tend to fail me, but I would recognize that *clomp* of orthopedic shoes anywhere." She went to the door and pulled it open. "Sister Kathleen! Is it you, dear?" She motioned to Clare to join her. "We gather in the next room."

As Clare stood up, she said, "I'm not sure I remember how to do this."

"It will come back to you quickly." Abigail turned her attention to the hallway. "Sister Kathleen," she called loudly. "Certainly that is you."

A moment passed. "Mercy sakes, Sister Abigail! The entire floor came to see what you're shouting about."

Abigail waved to the blurred figures in the hallway. "And may God bless each of them."

Clare followed the women into the next

room. The white walls were bare with the exception of a simple crucifix and a tall, metal supply cabinet.

"This is the workroom," Abigail said. "Throughout the day groups of Sisters labor here to provide the world with religious goods."

"Holy cards, vestments, rosaries." Sister Kathleen looked Clare over. "A couple of years ago we even had a nun who carved images of Christ in bars of soap. Are you visiting us today?"

"She is joining us," Abigail said as she moved toward a wooden table that was nearly as long as the room. "This week and every week."

"She can't do that."

"Of course she can."

Sister Kathleen put her hands on her hips. "We have six workstations and there are six of us."

"Sister Agnes is incapable of continuing in this ministry."

"I don't think filling her spot before she's passed on is in good taste. Nothing personal, Sister Clare. Sister Agnes has been with us for twelve years. You understand."

Monica walked over. "Who is this?"

Abigail put her hand on Clare's shoulder. "My new roommate. She will be joining us to make rosaries."

"What a joy," Monica said. "A new Sister!"

"I don't think it's right," Sister Kathleen said. "If Sister Agnes gets well we won't have room for her."

Patrice approached the table. "Agnes is heaven bound."

"We don't know that," Sister Kathleen argued.

"She has congestive heart failure that isn't responding to medication. She has a few days at the most. You know we could use the help."

"Abigail," Monica said, "you are going to introduce us."

"Are we all here?"

Patrice answered, "Graciella just arrived."

"Sisters, this wonderful new addition to our Tranquil Garden community is Sister Clare of the Sisters of the Sacred Heart. She worked among the dying. Sit down, everyone." Abigail waited until the sounds of chairs moving ceased. "Clare, to my left is Patrice from the Community of the Precious Blood."

"Retired nurse. Glad to have you with us."

"To the left of Patrice we have Monica from the Sisters of Loretto."

"I was a schoolteacher," she said softly. "English."

"And to the left of Monica," Abigail continued, "we have Sister Kathleen from the community of the Holy Family."

Sister Kathleen lowered her head and peered above her low-hanging glasses. "Bishop

Logan High School, principal for thirty-one years."

"And there beside you is Sister Graciella of the Sisters of the Incarnate Word. Graciella is our silent treasure."

"She speaks every so often," Patrice said. "And when she does, it's usually a good idea to listen."

"Graciella is spending her retirement years pondering the presence of our Lord," Abigail said lovingly. "She is the gentlest of all His creatures."

The quiet nun left her chair and walked over to Clare. She took hold of Clare's hands and bowed her head.

"What is she doing?" Sister Kathleen asked.

Graciella smiled as her soft brown eyes met Clare's. "Welcome, dear one," she said.

Sister Kathleen raised her eyebrows. "She never greeted me that way."

"Well, shall we get started?" Abigail asked. "Whose turn is it to pass out the supplies?"

"Mine," Monica answered. She hurried to the supply cabinet. "I will only be a minute."

"Where do the rosaries go from here?" Clare asked.

"Prisons, for the most part," Patrice said.

Sister Kathleen took a plastic box from Monica. "They wear them as jewelry. It's a disgrace, if you ask me."

"I didn't want to know that," Monica said with a moan. "They are tools of prayer, not jewelry."

"They are seeds," Abigail said. "Each time one is glanced upon, some man or woman sees the beloved face of Christ, and in the silent power of the Holy Spirit, the seed is planted."

"This is wrong," Sister Kathleen said strongly. "This is all wrong."

Patrice looked over. "What's the matter?"

"These beads are blue. I use the black beads. I always use black beads." She sighed heavily. "For ten years I have used only black beads and today she hands me blue."

"Black, blue," Patrice said, shaking her head. "What's the difference?"

Sister Kathleen pointed to the beads in front of Clare. "Those are my beads."

"You better give them to her, Clare," Patrice said sarcastically, "before she works herself into a stroke."

"Abigail," Monica said as she took her seat, "continue with the story you were telling us."

"And what story was that, dear?"

"The one about The Order."

"You left us hanging last week," Sister Kathleen said. "I don't like that."

"Does anyone remember where I left off?"

Monica uncoiled an arm-length of wire, which was used to connect the beads together.

"The Sisters of the Divine Name arrived to establish a foundation in New England in the year 1788. During that winter, an outbreak of influenza threatened to wipe out the entire community."

Sounding irritated, Sister Kathleen said, "All week I have been wondering what on earth happened to them."

"If they had been wiped out," Patrice said, "then Abigail would be sitting here wearing a different habit."

"You are a Sister of the Divine Name?" Clare asked.

"Professed seventy-two years ago. The Sisters of the Divine Name were formed some 750 years ago in France. Then in 1788—in order to avoid persecution—our Motherhouse was reestablished in America, in the Boston area."

"Who was persecuting it?" Patrice asked.

"Who is not the pressing question," said Abigail, "but *why."* She felt for a bead. "From its earliest history, the Divine Name had certain Sisters blessed by God with powerful spiritual gifts. Within the Divine Name community, God gathered these souls into a smaller group, a group referred to simply as The Order."

"Repeat the part, for Clare, where it was first formed," suggested Monica.

"That will take too long," Sister Kathleen complained.

"I will keep it brief." Abigail searched her

bag for another bead. "In the twentieth year of our history, the novitiate experienced an outpouring of the Holy Spirit unlike any other. One of the novices received the stigmata: her hands, her feet, and her side contained the visible wounds of Christ. As a result, she was taken to study directly with the Superior General, our founding mother. Each month that followed that first outpouring, the young saint walked into the novitiate and laid hands upon a different novice until The Order numbered twelve."

"Did they all have the stigmata, Abigail?" Monica asked.

"Only the one. But the gifts of the others were just as extraordinary. There were prophetic dreams, divine visions, miracles, gifts of healing, and others that my weak mind can not grasp or explain. They were experiences this religious has never known."

"I admire the discipline they must have had," Sister Kathleen said. "You can't maintain the spiritual life without it."

Abigail nodded. "They lived an austere lifestyle of sacrifice and prayer. We saw them only when the community shared the evening meal and when there was a need to seek spiritual direction."

"Explain to them the purpose," Graciella said.

"Purpose of what?" Patrice asked.

Graciella looked at Abigail. "The purpose

of The Order was known in many places. Tell them."

Abigail put down her pliers. "I wonder, Sisters, this may not be an appropriate story for our gatherings. It requires an openness of heart and of mind."

Sister Kathleen looked at Abigail over her glasses. "You can't stop now—you have us all interested."

"Very well." She cleared her throat. "Every word uttered by a person either adds to the light or adds to the darkness. Likewise, every deed. As you know, we human creatures all too often choose the easiest path."

"The one that leads to darkness," Sister Kathleen said.

"Hush," Patrice said. "Let Abigail tell it."

"The specifics of how it was to carry out its special calling or why it was contained to the number twelve—I can give no answers for that. The purpose of God is not entirely clear. What *is* clear is that Our Lord established The Order to do a work no other order was performing. The Order was chosen by our Great and Powerful God to be a beacon in the darkened days preceding His Son's return. To continually fulfill the words of the prophet Joel."

"'Your sons and daughters will prophesy,'" Sister Kathleen said quietly.

"'Your old will dream dreams,'" Patrice said.

Monica wiped a tear from her eye. "'Your young will see visions.'"

"For more than seven centuries not even deaths within The Order stopped that work of God," Abigail said. "Whenever one Sister was called from this life, another would be appointed. Months before one of The Order approached death, there would be a stirring of the Holy Spirit among the class of novices. Just as in the days of the early church, spiritual phenomena of every kind flooded the lives of the young women. It was the particular duty of the Mistress of Novices to discern which novice was actually being called. This was no simple task, because the powers of darkness were always present as well. For every gift of the Spirit there is a counterfeit gift. One spreads light and goodness, the other spreads darkness and evil."

Patrice clipped off a piece of wire. "What happened once she made the choice?"

"The Mistress of Novices, who was not of The Order herself, would escort the young nun to a room we called the Chamber of Waiting. Once inside, the novice would be asked a question by the perishing member of The Order. If she provided the correct answer, the dying member laid hands upon the chosen novice and recited the words of an ancient prayer, and the Order would continue."

"Did anyone ever give a wrong answer?" Monica asked.

"That, I do not know." Abigail picked up her pliers again. "But I do know that historians would enjoy comparing the atrocities of man against the prophecies entrusted to The Order. Had the nobles and kings of the day taken heed to the offered warnings, more than one dark and tragic event would have been erased from history."

"Tell us a prophecy," Patrice said.

"One small example would be the warning given to the monarch of France in 1779." She felt around her plastic bag for a bead. "The Order sent word that a time of trial would be felt across the land if certain measures were not taken to protect the French economy. The king refused to see beyond the plenty that filled his table. Ten years later, the financial crisis came and the French Revolution began. It was a time of turmoil, confusion, and anarchy that led many of the faithless and the faithful to the guillotine.

"But not all were lost," continued Abigail. "Before Divine Providence swept those of the Divine Name away to the safe harbor of America, The Order faithfully proclaimed the prophetic vision. Church leaders heard God's voice within the message and did what they could. As grave as the situation was, it would have been far worse had the prophetic vision not been entrusted to The Order."

"She's not doing it right," Sister Kathleen

said. "Her wire loops between the beads are too big."

Clare held up her work. "I'm a bit rusty at this."

"It's fine," Patrice said, looking sternly at Sister Kathleen. "Try using the tip of your pliers to make the loop in the wire instead of the middle."

"Please continue, Abigail," Monica said. "When did you say the Sisters came to America?"

"Half of them arrived on American soil in 1788 and were given a piece of property near Boston. The Sisters moved in and immediately began hiring laborers to build a house large enough to hold them along with the additional arrivals who would be coming in the spring, as the community continued fleeing Europe. One day a laborer fell ill and died in their care."

"And whatever illness he had, he gave to the Sisters," Patrice said. "They knew so little about protection from airborne disease in those days."

"That is precisely what happened," Abigail said. "The number of dead increased steadily as the harsh winter began. When spring arrived, a boat containing some thirty of our nuns made the crossing to America. These Sisters had been sent word of the disease and spent the entire winter fasting and praying for the survival of the ill. They were prepared to find the house empty of all life." Abigail placed her hand on Clare's forearm. "What time is it?"

She looked up, then answered. "A quarter till two."

"I must leave you now, Sisters."

"We have the room until two o'clock," Sister Kathleen said. "If you leave now, we'll be left hanging at the exact same spot you left us last week."

"Were any of the Sisters alive?" Monica asked worriedly. "Oh, I'm not sure I want to hear the answer."

Sister Kathleen shook her head. "I'm beginning to think she leaves us hanging on purpose."

"Abigail told us last week she was going to leave early to attend a devotional by the Daughters of the Immaculate Heart," Patrice said.

"And it is a lengthy walk from here to the sanctuary." Abigail smiled. "But I will conclude this episode with the good news that all twelve members of The Order and twelve additional Sisters were found alive and well." She pushed herself up from the table. "May I go to my devotional now?"

"One more question," Patrice said. "Is The Order still in place to this very day?"

Abigail's expression changed. "I think you will all agree that never has the world known a more darker age than the one we are in. Perversion and immorality run rampant. Greed motivates the hearts of the majority. Children are murdered in their schools. Parents are murdered in their workplaces." She made her way to the door, then turned and faced the table of nuns. "But what will come in the future we will not know. The powers of darkness struck again in the early 1940s. The blow appears to be permanent. Only one member of The Order still lives."

"You are going to tell us what happened?" Sister Kathleen asked.

Abigail raised her hand. "That part of the story, my dear children, will have to wait for another day."

Three

Room 142 of the northeast wing of the Tranquil Garden Nursing Home was dark with the exception of a thin strip of light beneath the door, seeping in from the perpetually lit hallway. Clare opened her eyes and waited in the now-familiar room. Throughout her life she had always been able to adjust to change quickly, and on this night—her third within this room—there was no forgetfulness of her current whereabouts nor any desire to return to former surroundings.

Filling the room were the sounds of Abigail's heavy breathing, but Clare was not disturbed by them as her waiting continued. The awakening at this late hour had been a call, one that was answered with the offering of a prayer, the prayer of patient waiting. And Clare knew this call would be followed by another, one that would require an action other than prayer. When the call would come—the exact hour and minute—would remain unknown to her, and there was peace in the not knowing, an all-encompassing peace that made the waiting an immeasurable pleasure.

The moments passed as the sounds of Abigail's sleeping continued. Then, in the gentle manner she had always known them to arrive, a second call came. It came without words that could be heard with ears of the flesh, but could be heard with inner ears that discerned only one voice, the voice of the One who always silently and lovingly guided her.

It was now time to leave. Moving her sock-covered feet out from beneath the covers, Clare got out of bed. As she reached for a thin robe, she felt around the tiled floor with her feet for a pair of fuzzy white slippers. Walking to the door, she pulled it open. Then Clare stepped carefully into the bright hallway.

Step after step she progressed toward her destination. Past the chapel, the dining room, the visiting area, and into the Critical Care Unit.

"What are you doing in here?" asked a brunette woman wearing a nurse's uniform. "Did you get lost?" The woman looked close at the nun. "Where do you want to go?"

Pointing at a door to the left, Clare said, "Inside that room."

The nurse checked her watch. "Visiting hours don't begin for three more hours."

Clare remained silent.

She studied the nun for a moment. "I guess it's all right. Go ahead, Sister."

Clare entered the room where Sister Agnes lay motionless. She moved a chair over near the bed and sat down.

"I was pretending to be asleep," said Sister Agnes quietly. "I thought you were a nurse."

"I'm not a nurse, only a friend."

"Do you hear singing?"

"It must be beautiful."

"Death is proving to be quite difficult. I seem to be stuck, my friend."

"Not stuck, precious one." Clare reached for the dying woman's hand. "I will wait with you."

"I dreamed of heaven before you came."

"Tell me your dream."

"I found myself in this place. It was unlike any other. Ice-like flooring stretched as far as I could see in all directions. Though it looked as if it should be cold, it was delightfully warm."

She paused until a wave of angina passed. "I felt no pain there. It's been many years since I've enjoyed such a pleasure. What is your name?"

"Clare."

"How grateful I am for such companionship."

"He provides our every need."

"His presence fills this room. It fills me. I can even feel it in my fingertips."

"You are almost home," Clare said. "He is drawing you to His side."

Sister Agnes raised her head slightly. "Do you see anything by the door?"

"I see a beautiful light."

"I want to get up and go into that light. But my body won't move."

"Then go in spirit. His longing is great." Clare kissed Sister Agnes's hand tenderly. "Go to Him."

Four

Did you fall asleep?" asked the nurse quietly as she gently rocked Clare's shoulder. "I need you to wake up so we can take care of Sister Agnes." She looked over at the deceased nun. "It must have been a gentle death; she looks so peaceful. It was good that you came when you did. We don't like any of them to die alone."

Daylight streamed in through the window. "It's morning," Clare said.

"Just after seven o'clock," the nurse answered. "You must be exhausted. Why don't I have someone wheel you back to your room?"

"No, that isn't necessary," Clare said, as she stood up stiffly.

She left the Critical Care Unit, and as she turned the corner, Clare saw that her path was blocked by a man slightly beyond middle age who was gracefully pushing a mop along the center section of the hallway. "Excuse me," she said.

He turned. "Yes, Sister?"

"Is there another way around? I don't

want to disturb your work, but I must get to the other side."

Putting his mop into the rolling bucket he said, "I always leave a strip for times just like this."

He took her arm. "I'll show you across." As they walked, he looked at her closely. "You must be one of the new Sisters?" She nodded. "Welcome to Tranquil Garden. I'm Tom. Floor Maintenance Executive since 1965."

"My name is Clare."

"It's a pleasure to meet you, Sister Clare. Here we go, just stay on the left."

"What is that smell?"

"I've been using a new disinfectant. You don't like it?"

"No, it's very pleasant. Lemon?" He answered her with a smile. "It's delightful."

"I know, these floor cleaners usually smell like medicine."

"Old medicine."

Tom laughed. "There you go, Sister Clare. You can walk on any part of the floor now."

"God bless you," she said softly.

He hesitated in letting go of her arm for a moment as he received the blessing. "Thank you, Sister." Tom released his steadying grip and watched the tiny figure, slightly bent with age, walk slowly down the hall.

Clare made another turn, leading her to room 142. "Good morning, Abigail."

"I'm glad you made it back from wherever you were," Abigail said with a hint of curiosity. "Nurse Gertie should be in any moment to check our vital signs. I have been trying to think of an excuse for your absence without committing sin."

"What would have happened if you simply said you didn't know?"

"It would be quite a scene indeed," said Abigail, taking on a serious tone. "Sirens would sound and flashing red lights would emerge through the roof tiles."

Clare began to laugh. Abigail joined her. Soon they both were going full-force. Then Clare placed her hand on her head. "Oh my goodness," she gasped. "I think I've laughed so hard I've made myself faint."

Abigail moved to her quickly. "You better sit down, child."

"It's been at least fifty years since some-one called me *child*. It has a delightful ring to it."

"Let's put you on the bed. How old are you?"

"Seventy-eight," she answered.

"I am ninety-two, and at my age most everyone is child to me."

Clare searched Abigail's nearly sightless eyes. "I imagine it has always been that way for you, regardless of your age."

"Yes, I guess it has. My first spiritual di-

rector explained my vow of chastity as giving up
the privilege of being a mother to some, in order
to be a mother to all. It struck me very deeply."
She guided Clare to the edge of the bed. "We've
known each other. I am certain of it, but I am
more certain that you already know how we
knew each other."

"Shall I tell you?"

"No, I enjoy a good mystery. It will come to
me." She thought for a moment. "Was it the
1959 seminar on contemplative prayer in Atlanta?"

"I've never been to Atlanta."

"Sisters, I have some news," said Nurse
Gertie with a sullen expression on her face.
Pushing her medicine cart into the room, she
looked at each Sister as if to ascertain whether
they would be strong enough to handle the information. "How are we feeling today?"

"Nurse Gertie?" Abigail inquired. "What's
wrong?"

"We—we lost Sister Agnes this morning."

"Have you told Sister Margaret?" Abigail
leaned over to Clare and whispered, "They were
like mother and daughter."

"Sister Janice is with her now." After she
had taken their blood pressure and recorded
the numbers on her clipboard, the pear-shaped
woman said, "We'll see you this afternoon, Sisters."

Clare went into the bathroom to dress

and prepare for the day. When she came out, she was wearing a modified habit, which looked like a parochial school uniform. "May I borrow a hair pin? One of mine just went down the sink."

"We wouldn't want your headpiece sliding off in the middle of breakfast." Abigail pointed to an unadorned bureau. "Top drawer, small dish on the left."

Abigail waited while Clare located a pin and secured her headwear. "We should start on our way to the dining room. You must be quite hungry after your pre-dawn expedition. What did you tell me was the work you did while you were in community?"

Clare offered her arm to Abigail. She had noticed that the older woman had particular struggles maneuvering the hallways with a number of people around, so she had made the gesture customary from her very first day. "I was a companion to the dying."

"Then it would be no great guess for me to assume you were with Sister Agnes this morning. And it would be no great revelation for you to answer that you were."

"I was with Agnes, if you were asking."

"Certainly not," Abigail said firmly. "I would never pry into your private affairs." They turned into the east/west hallway. "But I am glad to hear it. If you were simply a late-night wanderer, you would be moved upstairs where a better eye could be kept on you. If that were to happen, I would be given another new roommate, and I don't want another roommate." Clare remained silent. "That was a compliment, child."

"One I appreciate."

"Indeed you should," said Abigail as they entered the dining room. "I am very picky."

"Clare! Abigail!" said someone with urgency. "Join our table this morning."

"Is that Monica I hear?" Abigail asked.

Clare looked around. "Yes, and Graciella is with her."

"Motion to her that we will join them."

A middle-aged man waited for Abigail to move her tray down the metal rails to his serving station. He, like most of the servers and kitchen help, was a volunteer from the local parish. "Oatmeal this morning, Sister Abigail?"

"Yes, Robert," she answered. "Go light on the butter and give me a full ladle of that delicious maple syrup."

"Warmed just for you, Sister." He prepared the bowl and passed it under the glass shield. "And what can I get for you this morning, Sister Clare?" he asked as he turned to her.

"I would like some of those scrambled eggs and several strips of that bacon."

Robert nodded and filled the plate. "Here you go, Sister."

Clare moved down the line, trying not to let the number of choices overwhelm her.

"Carry your tray, Sister?" asked a young man whose head was covered with a mound of brown curls.

"I believe I can manage this time," she replied. Her orange juice swayed in the glass as she walked over to the table.

"We were talking about Sister Agnes. How quickly our prayers that she no longer be in such pain were answered," Monica said as Clare unloaded her tray. "She could have suffered for weeks and months. Instead, she is in paradise at this very moment."

"I wish it were me," Abigail said. "It is difficult when you have lived a life of service."

"You still serve," Monica insisted.

"Not in the way that I was trained, dear." She stirred her oatmeal. "One would think that after more than fifteen years of retirement I would be fully adjusted and rejoice in my hours of leisure."

Noticing Clare watch as Graciella scraped butter from her toast, Monica said, "Graciella always has two pieces of dry toast for breakfast. Sometimes they forget. She won't eat it with anything on it." Her voice quieted to a whisper. "It's one of her peculiar ways."

"I was told there was going to be a craft lesson tomorrow early afternoon," Abigail said. "Monica, I assume you are going."

"We are going to assemble birdhouses from kits and paint them ourselves. Sister Kathleen is coming. Why don't you both join us?"

"I am not very handy with a hammer," Abigail said.

"No hammers. The pieces fit together. It will be like building a simple model plane." Monica reached for her coffee. "The real fun is going to be the painting."

"Although it does sound interesting, I will have to decline," Abigail said. "Tomorrow morning I am having a visitor."

"Visitors!" Monica brought her hands together. "How delightful. Who are they?"

"A Sister from my community is flying in to see me. How I wish I could convince her to take me back to Massachusetts, but these lungs of mine need warm air, and it is still many weeks before the first hints of spring in the north." Abigail gathered another spoonful of oatmeal and sighed. "Words can not express the wonderful fragrance of warmed maple syrup."

Clare lifted a strip of bacon from her plate. "Monica, is everything all right?"

"Yes, no. I'm—I'm fine."

"You're frightened," Abigail said. "I can hear it in your voice. Is it the same thing that has been troubling you in recent times?"

Monica looked around the crowded room. "There's so much I don't understand, and I'm not sure I would want to understand this even if I could."

Abigail put down her spoon. "And what are you not understanding?"

"Something is terribly wrong. Someone among us is terribly wrong—is trying to hurt us. Why?

To Clare, Abigail said, "Monica has a sensitivity to spiritual forces. As you can see, this special gift also is a burden, because it includes distinguishing evil. The presence of someone walking in darkness is unsettling to Monica."

Turning to Monica, Clare said, "Take comfort in this, Sister: The torment they must be going through surrounded by so many who love Our Lord is much greater than the discomfort you are suffering."

"I know you're right, but it grows stronger by the day." Monica closed her eyes. "What could the dark powers want here?"

"What evil wants in any place," Clare said, "to destroy the loving trust between a soul and God."

Pushing her bowl away, Abigail said, "We must be firm in faith, Sisters. It seems that a time of testing may be coming upon us."

Five

When Sister Janice walked into the special events room of the Tranquil Garden Nursing Home, she saw that each table had been meticulously prepared for the event of the day. But she took it upon herself to double-check and make sure everything on the newspaper-covered tables was in place.

Mother Francesca came into the room. Her dark hair and unwrinkled face hid the fact that she was well past the secular world's age of retirement.

"Everything seems to be in order," Mother Francesca said.

Sister Janice looked up. "I've double-checked all the tables."

"Tell me, how are our new residents adjusting?"

"All three Sisters seem to be doing fine: Sister Florence will be in the class today. Sister Gloria is having a bit of a strain with her arthritis medications, but I think it has been worked out. And I will be seeing Sister Clare shortly when I read to Sister Abigail."

Mother Francesca reached into her pocket and pulled out a folded piece of paper. She handed it to Sister Janice. "I have been informed that Sister Meredith was found walking outside the gate. Do you know anything about it?"

"She often walks in the mornings, but she knows not to leave the property."

"I'm afraid that one day soon she will. Please make sure that one of our staff is given the task of keeping a constant eye on her."

"Yes, Mother."

The room filled slowly with residents and volunteers. Sister Kathleen, Monica, and Florence were gathered as a group and led to a table.

"They usually give us nametags," Monica said. "I'm Monica, and this is Sister Kathleen."

"My name is Florence, of the Sisters of the Sacred Heart."

Monica's eyes widened. "Our friend Clare is also from the Sisters of the Sacred Heart."

"Yes, we arrived together. I miss her and Gloria terribly."

"Who's Gloria?" Sister Kathleen asked.

"She's also from our convent and arrived here with us. I haven't seen either of them since we got here. After all those years in community, you would think they would let us stay together, but no, they whisked us away in separate directions. I don't even know where either of them are."

Monica smiled warmly. "Clare mentioned at breakfast that she was having difficulty finding you. Her room number is 142. Why don't you go by sometime and let her know where you are?"

"They don't let me go anywhere without an escort."

Sister Kathleen put her elbows on the table and leaned forward. "Your room must be on the second floor."

"How did you know?"

"That's where they keep—" Monica nudged her firmly. "They just take extra care of the residents up there."

"I don't like being here," said Florence with a trembling voice.

Lowering her head and peering above her brown-rimmed glasses, Sister Kathleen said, "It takes some getting used to, but once you find a few new ways to minister and a companion or two, it won't seem so bad."

"There is an evil in this place; *that* is what makes it seem so bad," said Florence firmly.

Keeping her voice low, Sister Kathleen said, "What are you talking about?"

"I will say no more here, Sisters. But pray: Pray without ceasing, and not for me or my transition here, but for this place and the one walking these halls who will be ruthless in carrying out plans for destruction."

"Sisters!" Sister Janice called loudly. "Mother Francesca is ready to begin."

As Mother Francesca began giving out patient instructions, Monica and Florence exchanged concerned glances. Then Florence closed her eyes, relieved. Monica knew. She was no longer alone.

Sister Janice noticed the time and silently dismissed herself. Compulsively punctual, she quickened her pace to room 142 in order to arrive on time.

"Sister Abigail, Sister Clare, good afternoon."

"My visitor has not arrived," Abigail said with concern.

"Visitor? I don't know of any visitor. Whom were you expecting?"

"One of the Sisters from my convent wrote me a letter saying that she would arrive today, this morning—at ten o'clock."

"You must be mistaken," Sister Janice said gently. "Those plans are always made through the main desk. I would know if anyone from your community was visiting today. Could you have your dates mixed up?"

"I must." For a moment Abigail remained quiet. "My mind is not suited for Jane Austen this afternoon. Would you read me something else today?"

"Anything you like."

"A selection from the Gospel of John would be nice, the twentieth chapter."

Sister Janice took a Bible from a bookcase near the bathroom and reverently read the sacred words of the Gospel. She allowed a time of silence. "Would you like for me to read another selection?"

"I think I would like to lie down before the Sisters arrive to make rosaries."

Returning the Bible to the shelf, Sister Janice said, "Then I will see you both next week."

After the sounds of the young woman's hard-soled shoes had faded, Clare noted her roommate's expression. "Something is wrong."

"Wrong? Possibly. Strange—definitely." Getting up from her chair, Abigail groped her way to the night table between the two beds. She opened the drawer and pulled out several pieces of stationery. "Will you find the passage of this letter that tells when Alicia intends to arrive?"

Clare read through the letter, then answered, "January twenty-fifth at ten in the morning."

"And what day is today?"

"January the twenty-fifth."

Abigail lifted her glasses and pinched the bridge of her nose. "I knew Sister Kathleen had not made a mistake in reading it to me. Read the portion preceding the expected date."

"It says: 'Our dear Sister Catherine died on the evening of January twentieth. She left a final word of prophecy, which she advised be given to you upon my arrival to Tranquil Garden.'"

"Sister Catherine was the last living member of The Order," explained Abigail. Her hands shook as she adjusted her glasses. "The ramifications of this news are not only great for The Order, but for the Sisters of the Divine Name, and also for the greater church. Her passing concludes a harsh devastation wrought by our spiritual enemies." She shook her head slowly. "I must know if it is all truly ended. I must know what the final prophecy is. A phone! We must get to a phone. Come with me quickly."

"Of course I will come, but I am afraid I can no longer do anything quickly."

"And I am even slower." She took hold of Clare's arm. "We will do the best we can. Our destination is the dining room."

They walked up the hallway and turned the corner. Clare saw Sister Janice sitting at her desk in the visitor's lounge. Her back was turned to them.

As they entered the dining room, Clare said, "Why are we here?"

"Sometimes I hear workers talking on the phone when we come for lunch, and I am certain that behind the serving line we will find a phone mounted to the wall. Take me there."

Clare searched the back wall as she escorted Abigail around the serving line. "There is one." She reached for the receiver. "Here."

"Dial 0." As Clare pushed the button, Abigail listened. "Something is wrong. Nothing is happening."

"No ringing?"

"None. It must be broken."

"Let me try something else." Clare cleared the line, then pushed another button. "What is it doing now?"

"I hear a dial tone. What did you do?"

"Business phones often require dialing 9 to get an outside line." She pushed zero. "There."

"It's ringing. Yes, operator—I would like to make a collect call to the Sisters of the Divine Name Convent in—what? But I don't have the number. That's why I'm calling you."

"Abigail!" Sister Janice said with surprise as she entered the dining hall. "I thought you were tired. What are you doing here?"

Her heart began to pound. "I—I don't know," responded Abigail.

Eying the receiver in Abigail's hand, she said, "All calls are supposed to go through my desk. You know that. You weren't about to use that, were you?" When Abigail did not answer, she said, "I don't want to see you put on phone restriction or have to bring this up with Mother Francesca. But if you don't tell me what is going on, I'll be left with no choice."

"I wanted to call my convent."

"Still worried over your missing visitor?" Sister Janice wrapped her arm around Abigail and began leading her out of the dining room. "I just got off the phone with your convent. There is a terrible snowstorm in the Northeast that has grounded all air travel. Sister Alicia will be delayed a few days."

"But she is coming?"

"She is, and I reminded her to call me from the airport when she arrives so that I can have a visitor's pass waiting for her." They reached the hallway. Sister Janice motioned to another nun to bring over a wheelchair. "Now, I want you to let Sister Josephine take you back to your room. Sister Clare, would you like for me to have someone take you back?"

Clare shook her head. "Please, allow me to escort Abigail."

Sister Janice dismissed Sister Josephine with a nod. "Now remember, I don't want to see either of you here again except during mealtimes."

Clare began pushing the wheelchair down the hallway. She noticed the old woman's shaking hands. "You're still troubled."

"A condition that will not lift until I hear the words of the final prophecy."

Six

I have to stop a minute," said Sister Kathleen. "These darn feet of mine."

Monica helped her to a chair. "I'll call a nurse."

"You will not." She sat down. "I can make it. I just need to sit a minute or two."

"But something might be wrong."

"I'm not going to do anything that gets me kicked off the ambulatory ward." She leaned back in the chair. "We both know how it works around here: You stay on the first floor until you can't walk; then they move you upstairs with the mentally deficient, where you sit around in your room until it's time for Critical Care. I still have a sharp mind and no serious illnesses, so I don't have to worry. But on days like today, that second floor is getting too close."

"Maybe it's those heavy shoes you wear. Sometime you should try wearing tennis shoes like I do. They are very comfortable."

"Tennis shoes while clothed in the habit? Never."

Monica glanced at a resident being escorted by a nurse to the elevator. "Isn't that Florence?"

"Going back upstairs. I don't envy her. I've heard some of them scream off and on for no reason."

Monica shuddered. "That can't be true."

"I wonder how many like Sister Florence are up on the second floor seeing a demon behind everything that happens. I've come across her kind before. Some of their stories can be unsettling."

"Some of their stories might be true."

Sister Kathleen got up with a groan. "What's that supposed to mean?"

"I think Florence senses something. Something real and frighteningly dark at work in one of us."

"Sister, in all my years I have never seen anyone full of the devil. I worked with teenagers, and if the devil could grab hold anywhere, they would make the easiest target."

"I have seen it, once."

Sister Kathleen reached for the handrail and began to walk. "When?"

"Years ago. I was visiting family back in Portland. We went to a Sunday service at a church known to welcome the homeless into the congregation. After the service I went to greet the priest. A destitute woman came up to me. Her clothes were tattered, but she had a loving smile. In those days my congregation still wore the habit, and she was taken with it."

"That doesn't sound like someone full of the devil."

"I first noticed something different about her eyes. They were so empty. I began feeling uncomfortable, but it was too late." Monica stopped walking. She began to cry softly.

"I have a tissue," Sister Kathleen said. "Come on now, it was a long time ago."

"It always seems like it just happened. The feeling comes back so strong." She wiped her eyes. "Her face contorted with such anger, and that horrible voice, I will never forget it."

"What did it say?"

"I hate you," she sobbed.

"Mercy sakes, Monica! That thing was speaking to the Lord, not you."

"I know." She wiped her eyes again. "I stood there frozen in fear."

"Who wouldn't have."

"In my heart I was proclaiming my love for Him, but the words wouldn't leave my mouth. I felt like, in some way, I betrayed Him."

"You just forget that nonsense. The Lord hears our thoughts. He knows what you wanted to say."

They began walking again.

"I wouldn't repeat that story too often,"

Sister Kathleen said. "You never know what might get you transferred to the second floor."

"Sister Kathleen!" Abigail called from the workroom further up the hallway. "Is that you, dear?"

Sister Kathleen moaned as she headed toward the room. "Must she always do that? She draws the attention of everyone on the floor."

"Sister Kathleen?" Abigail called again. "Are you there?"

"Everyone is looking at me."

"No, they aren't," said Monica.

"Yes, they are, Sister."

Monica looked at the faces in the doorways as they walked. "You're right. They are."

"And how does she know I'm coming?" Sister Kathleen raised her hand in the air and waved toward Abigail several times: "See that? Abigail can't see a thing. How does she know that it's me? Why is she never shouting out your name, or any of the others?"

"I don't know, Sister."

"I think a prolonged death would be easier to take than these weekly displays."

"Good afternoon, Sister Kathleen," Abigail said. "We are all waiting inside except for Monica."

"I am here, Abigail."

"Oh—good afternoon, dear, come on inside." She took hold of Sister Kathleen's hand. "I have some disappointing news. The new shipment of supplies arrived. The black beads, however, were not included as requested."

"No black beads?" said a disappointed Sister Kathleen.

Monica pulled her chair out from the table. "You could make a blue rosary."

"I make black rosaries with black beads. That's how it has been for sixty years, and how it will stay." Her face flushed. "I think I'll just go back to my room."

"But you can't," Monica insisted. "Abigail's story. Please, sit with us."

"I don't have anything to do."

Patrice began passing out pliers. "You can supervise."

"Go on," urged Monica. "Sit." She smiled at Clare, then looked at Abigail. "We're ready to hear the story."

"Where did I leave off last time?"

"Something happened to cause The Order's number to fall below twelve," Patrice said.

Abigail picked up a bead. "It was a time when all of Europe trembled as the Nazi war machine began its campaign of terror. The shadow of darkness seemed to be cast throughout the whole of Europe. Jews were being massacred by the tens of thousands. Every atrocity was being committed openly. But here in America, far from the reaches of Nazi bombs, all seemed calm."

"She's only got nine beads there," Sister Kathleen said, pointing at Clare's work. "It's not a decade without ten beads before the chain separator."

Patrice checked Clare's beads. "I count ten. Monica?"

"They are all there."

"Then I apologize, Sister Clare."

"Back to the story," Patrice said. "Go ahead, Abigail."

"The convents of the Sisters of the Divine Name in Europe did what they could to help those escape who were targeted by Nazi hatred. But it became the special task of our sisters in Belgium to provide sanctuary to Jews and resistance fighters.

"Early in the war, they were able to secure safe passage for many Jews to leave the country. Word spread throughout the underground, gaining them a tremendous reputation. After the Nazis sealed every possible way out of the country, the Sisters continued in their dangerous work of providing food and temporary shelter to any refugees that came their way."

"I can't even imagine what those years must have been like for many people," Monica said. It's all so horrible."

Sister Kathleen nodded her head. "We sure were lucky on this side of the ocean. Other than using a ration book, I never would have known there was a war on."

Abigail cleared her throat. "But then a time came when they could no longer offer assistance of any kind. One of the Sisters from that convent was a dear friend of mine. She wrote me letters detailing the struggles they faced under the strain of living in an occupied country."

"My grandparents lived through the war in England," Patrice said. "They never got over it."

"Those things have to be left in the Lord's hands," Sister Kathleen said. "What happened in the past should stay there."

"In 1940 she wrote to us about a young family," Abigail continued, "who underwent a perilous journey to escape the Nazis. The mother was Jewish, the father, a French gentile. Their children ranged in age from seven to fifteen years. The Nazis were closing in on many countries in Europe. Our convent was nestled in the countryside, making the Sisters of the Divine Name their last hope of securing sanctuary and avoiding arrest. My friend held the job of answering the door, and although their plight was serious and life threatening, she was bound by obedience. She turned the family away."

Monica's eyes filled with tears. "She didn't."

"Obedience is hardest when the result is not within the present," Abigail said. "During those years we at the Motherhouse in Westbury

experienced more sickness and death among
The Order than at any other time in our history."

"But you said the Lord always brought up
another sister to replace the one who was dying
in The Order," Patrice said.

"And He did. Just after the war, in 1946, a
mysterious illness brought Sister Dominique
into her final days. There at the Motherhouse
various spiritual gifts fell upon the members of
the novitiate class. It would be the third class in
a row requiring a novice to be called. As I said,
the Holy Spirit fell, but two stood out from the
rest. The first young girl was named Rachel
Aames. She was an extraordinary contemplative, quite advanced in prayer. It was the custom of our community for each postulant to
select a consecrated name just prior to profession of first vows. Therefore we referred to her
as Novice Rachel."

"*Ours* came prior to entrance," Sister
Kathleen said. "From the earliest days of our
postulancy through Vatican II and into today,
we address a religious as *Sister,* and we always
wear the habit."

"A habit and a name doesn't make you a
religious," Patrice said. "It's your commitment
and devotion to Jesus."

"And that is shown through how you present yourself to the world." Sister Kathleen

tugged on her habit. "I am saying I belong to the Lord."

"We kept our baptismal names," Patrice said. "And I've never felt like I missed out on anything."

"I don't even want to remember my baptismal name," Monica said. "I never cared for it."

"What was it?" Clare asked. "Tell us."

"It was—it was Elma."

Sister Kathleen lowered her head and looked over the edge of her glasses. "There's nothing wrong with Emma."

"I agree, but I didn't say *Emma,* I said *Elma.*"

"My mother's name happened to be Elma," Sister Kathleen said.

"Sisters," Clare said. "We should let Abigail get back to the story."

"And I shall." She reflected briefly. "The second girl was Genevieve de Chantal. Like many of that class, Genevieve arrived in America following the war. She displayed a gift unlike any other: the ability to draw others to the state of union with the Lord while in prayer. Without effort on her part, other souls would be led inward and receive unfathomable consolations. I can't tell you how often the Superior General found dozens of nuns lying about the floor of the chapel. They seemed to collapse from the sheer joy of it."

Patrice asked, "What was Rachel's gift?"

"She began having heavenly visions."

"A visionary," Monica whispered.

"I myself was present once as she beheld a glimpse of the divine. Her countenance changed entirely, but not in a way that would draw attention to herself. The palms of her hands became coated with what looked like sweat, but was thick like anointing oil, and smelled of myrrh."

"Which one went into The Order?" Sister Kathleen asked.

Abigail snipped off a piece of wire. "As the days of Sister Dominique's life drew to a close, both young women continued to experience their gifts—which had never happened before. All other gifts of the novitiates diminished except for the gifts of the one anointed to enter The Order."

"Now I'm sure that section doesn't have ten beads, Sister Clare," Sister Kathleen said.

"There's ten," Patrice said sharply. "Stop interrupting. Clare knows what she's doing."

"It was left to the Mistress of Novices to make the selection, since she had supervised the studies of the young women and provided their spiritual direction. The choice held great danger. She believed that one of them had fallen victim to a counterfeit gift. The wrong choice would gain the serpent a stronghold among the twelve."

Sister Kathleen said, "Not a choice I would volunteer to make."

"Because Genevieve held a gift that affected others so profoundly, she was chosen. She took on the name *Sister Theresa* and was taken to the Chamber of Waiting. Alone, she stood before the bed of Sister Dominique. Alone, she received the mantle of graces and became one of the twelve."

"So nothing changed," Sister Kathleen said. "The Order continued."

"Actually, a tremendous change had taken place. The powers of darkness had infiltrated The Order."

Monica brought her hand to her mouth. "Sister Theresa?"

Abigail nodded. "A young girl bent on revenge."

"For what?" Patrice asked.

"It had been Sister Theresa on the porch of our convent in Belgium. It was her father who pleaded so earnestly for sanctuary. Within days of leaving our grounds, the entire family had been arrested. The parents were executed. The children were sent to concentration camps, with the exception of Genevieve. And only because her lovely face and maturing body caught the eye of an influential official, did she alone survive."

"She blamed the Sisters of the Divine Name," Monica said.

"Her tragic wound opened a window to the powers of darkness. Destroying the Sisters of the Divine Name was the only thing that would quench her thirst for revenge. To do that she would have to destroy not only the Mother-house, but The Order. A mission she began the day she left Europe for America in early 1944."

"I can't believe none of you knew," Sister Kathleen said.

"There was no evidence in the beginning, but the Mistress of Novices began witnessing events that caused her to realize she had made a dreadful mistake in selecting Sister Theresa. To admit poor discernment was not something that she intended to do. The woman suffered greatly from the fault of pride. Her outer appearance radiated a humble servant of Christ, but her inner condition was quite another story. She was mortified over the idea of the entire community discovering her mistake."

Monica asked, "How did she know she made the wrong choice?"

"Novice Rachel continued to receive heavenly visions. That in itself should have brought the matter to the Superior General, but it was the behavior of Sister Theresa that convinced her." She put her pliers down. "The newest member of The Order was supposed to be living a cloistered life of deep prayer. But the Mistress of Novices began catching Sister Theresa in prayer with other novices—only she was no longer leading them to the Lord, she was drawing them to herself. Her spiritual gift was one filled with danger. Used for good, it would be an invaluable tool of intercession as those drawn in were referred to Christ Jesus. Used for evil, the gift was capable of destroying souls and bending the will to acts of evil."

"That was your best one yet, Sister Abigail," Sister Kathleen said. She looked around the table. "Come on with these frightened faces. It isn't a real story." She looked around the table again. "Right, Abigail?"

"She speaks the truth," Graciella said.

"Sister Theresa continued on the path of the counterfeit gifts. Eventually it led her—and a few others who were drawn into her ensnaring darkness—down the path to murder."

The room fell silent.

Abigail tapped Clare's arm. "Could you tell me the time?"

"It's five minutes after two o'clock," Patrice said. "But you can't stop now. Tell us about the murder."

Sister Kathleen leaned over toward Monica. "Now I'm sure she leaves us hanging on purpose."

Abigail stood up. "Until next week, Sisters."

Seven

Clare entered the chapel unaware that she had neglected to exchange her fuzzy white slippers for more standard foot apparel. There was no service to attend this morning; she made the journey for the sole purpose of seeking solitude. Life at the Tranquil Garden Nursing Home had been pleasant enough, but it lacked the privacy she had been given while living in community with the Sisters of the Sacred Heart. The convent had provided precious hours of solitude both in the morning and evening hours, but here, so far, she had only managed a few stolen minutes.

Near the front of the chapel, she situated herself on a pew. The ceiling and stained glass windows resembled any other sanctuary she had ever visited, but the life-sized crucifix mounted to the wall behind the altar was unlike any she had ever seen before. The Christ's expression was so real, so pained.

Clare noticed a figure approaching from

her right. She turned her head slightly to see Graciella coming quietly toward her. She gave a smile of welcome as the tiny nun sat down beside her.

"You should be at breakfast," Graciella said softly.

"And so should you."

"Shall I leave you to your prayer, dear one?"

Clare shook her head. "Stay." She looked to the wooden-bead rosary hanging down from Graciella's belt. "I will recite the rosary with you."

"This is not my form of prayer," confided Graciella. "Like all religious in my community, I wear the rosary as part of my habit, but I was not blessed with the ability to use it as a tool of prayer."

Clare sighed in relief. "I wasn't either. What then is your tool of prayer?"

"Life." She smiled. "I find Our Lord there, in every facet."

Clare closed her eyes. The minutes passed steadily. As the time for breakfast ended, the chapel doors opened and the sanctuary filled with the shuffling sounds of nuns arriving for one devotional or another. Leaving Graciella, Clare walked into the hallway. At the glass door that led to the back courtyard, she stopped.

"Good morning, Abigail," said Clare.

"Come and sit with me on this beautiful day of sunshine our Lord has provided for us." Clare took a seat next to her on a wooden bench. "I missed you at breakfast. Were you on another excursion of mercy?"

"No, but I will tell you where I was, if you are asking."

"I am not. I would never pry into your private affairs." Abigail patted Clare's hand. "I could never bear these long days without my little rests in this courtyard. The noise of the city I can do without, but the noise of nature is my delight. What do you hear?"

"Birds."

"Is that all?"

"Waves rolling onto the beach. And something else." She listened closely. "I don't know what that is."

"That is the sound of the wind moving the tall blades of grass on the other side of the gate." Abigail got up. "Come with me."

Clare followed her to an iron gate at the edge of the courtyard and opened it.

"I can not see it, but you should find a substantial clump of high grasses somewhere near."

"They're here. I see them."

"Watch the blades dance as the wind directs them. That is the whole of the spiritual life; to bend to the wind of the Holy Spirit as easily as those blades bend to the wind of the earth." Abigail breathed deeply. "I am feeling a surge of energy. See the Gulf of Mexico out there? I intend to make a visit."

"You want to walk down to the beach?"

"Indeed, I think I will."

"But shouldn't we ask someone?"

"If we ask someone, child, they will strap large floating devices to our backs, and half the staff will accompany us to make sure we don't so much as dent the sand. If you would like to come, come. Otherwise I will see you later."

Clare and Abigail headed toward the sandy beach with the swiftness of turtles. A detour had to be made here and there as they found their way around the retaining wall, but they managed to reach the shore unscathed. The strong wind brought up waves that left behind a foamy residue. The two women stopped and let the sound of the gulf fill their ears. To the left, a pair of seagulls gathered just overhead. To the right, a seemingly endless shoreline stretched to Mexico.

Abigail closed her eyes and welcomed the warm breeze. "How I long to return home."

"We are already into February; March will come quickly."

"I don't mean *home* as in community, I mean *home* as in *Home*. I long for heaven."

"It will come soon enough."

"I ponder my lingering here. I wonder what purpose it serves for me to remain while this body continues to dwindle in efficiency." She leaned heavily on Clare as her balance temporarily gave way. "But I do not see as God sees. For instance, I only see the sand as all white. But there must be various hues? Speckles? Tones? What do you see?"

"The wet sand is one color: a gentle brown. The dry sand is nearly white."

"How I miss the sight of a sandy beach, of most everything, but I will not complain. My precious blurs are blessings compared to total blindness."

"Do the glasses help?"

"Not one bit. I've been wearing one pair or another for more than seventy years. Putting them on is as automatic for me as putting on my shoes." Abigail laughed. "More truthfully, my appearance is rather frightening without them, so I allow myself the one vanity."

"Please take them off," Clare said. "And let me see."

"You have been fairly warned," said Abigail as she removed her glasses. "See?"

"Not frightening, Abigail," Clare said as she stroked the elder nun's cheek. "Beautiful."

"I am certain I know you." She thought for a moment. "Could we have met in Chicago?"

"I've never been to Chicago."

"It's a remarkable place. They call it the windy city, although it was not at all windy during my short stay there."

"Sister Clare!" A loud voice called from behind the women. "Sister Abigail!"

Clare turned. "It's Sister Janice."

"I think we are in trouble," said Abigail.

"Sisters, what are you doing here?"

"We are standing," Clare answered.

Attempting to hide her smile, Abigail said, "Indeed, we are standing."

"Breaking the rules is never funny."

Abigail lowered her head. "No, Sister."

"Where are you going, Sister Clare?" Sister Janice asked.

"Back to my room."

"Please wait here until Mother Francesca and Sister Josephine arrive with the wheelchairs."

"There's no need. I can walk."

"Falls are serious. We will not risk any fractures today, Sisters." She looked up. "Here comes Mother. I hope you both have good reasons for disregarding the safety rules here."

Mother Francesca walked onto the sandy beach. "Are they injured?"

"No," Sister Janice answered.

"How did they get here?"

"I don't know."

"I asked Clare to bring me," Abigail said. "We walked."

Mother Francesca wrapped her arm around Abigail and began escorting her to the wheelchair waiting at the edge of the beach. "You know that no one is to go beyond the courtyard without permission."

"I forgot."

"Did you?" Mother Francesca asked in a loving tone. "Or did you simply wish to go?"

"I wanted to go."

"The mind is sound and the spirit is as feisty as it was last year." She guided Abigail around a piece of debris that had washed up during high tide. "There are a thousand dangers between here and the safety of Tranquil Garden. Had Sister Clare not been with you, you could have walked straight off the retaining wall and fallen to your death. I want you to understand how serious this violation of the rules is. Please tell me there's no need to put you on added watch with the staff."

Abigail shook her head. "No. No need."

"Good. Then we will hear no more about this."

Eight

A refrigerated truck was pulling into the delivery entrance of the Tranquil Garden Nursing Home. Doug Brennan sat behind the wheel. His receding brown hair and sun-worn face made him look much older than his thirty-six years. But Doug was unaware of any lacking in his appearance. His wife and his daughters thought he was handsome, and so, without question, he knew he was.

He drove up the driveway until his front bumper tapped the trash dumpster, then he shifted into reverse and backed up to the landing. "This can't be Friday," he announced to the man approaching him. "I still have some of my paycheck left."

A wiry man with a toothy smile waved. "It's still Monday as far as I know, but what do I know?"

"Robert here on a Monday, this is a first," said Doug.

"Just helping out."

"When do you get paid to work?"

Robert smiled as he pushed wire-rimmed glasses back up the bridge of his nose. "I'll get into the office around ten o'clock; once everything from breakfast is washed and put away."

"Then you must be the boss or something."

"It's a tough life."

"I bet." Doug wiped dirt from his eye. "The last three weeks haven't been too tough for me."

"Where did you go on that vacation?"

"San Antonio."

"Nice?"

"Yeah, but it's good to be back." He sat on the rear bumper. "Hey, just to let you know, they changed my delivery schedule. I'll be coming here Mondays and Thursdays."

"As of when?" Robert asked.

"As of this week."

"Does Mother Francesca know about this?"

"Not yet."

Robert removed his glasses and rubbed his eyebrow. "We'll have to change the amounts we order. It's going to be a lot of work for somebody."

Doug pulled open the heavy doors of the refrigerated truck. "As long as it's not you or me."

At that, both men laughed. As they began unloading the truck, Doug checked several boxes against his invoice. He placed them on a utility dolly. "Think she'll take one more?"

Robert took hold of the rubber handles and leaned the dolly back. "You better carry that one."

Doug followed Robert toward the nursing home entrance. As soon as he walked into the entrance, an overwhelming wave of anxiety swept over him, causing his heart to pound within his chest. His vision became blurred by black spots as if he were about to pass out. He put the box down and wiped the sweat from his hands. He walked back outside.

Robert came back out with the empty dolly. "The boxes go inside, remember?" The man nodded. "Hey, are you all right?"

Doug shook his head as if trying to shake something loose. "I don't think I feel so good."

He bent down to pick up the box. "I had an extra cup of coffee this morning. I guess I just got too wired." He went inside and set the box down on the floor. He looked around the storage room. "This is weird."

"What?"

"I'm not sure. My heart's pounding like I'm scared half to death."

"Are you scared?"

Doug began to breathe hard. "Yeah."

"Of what?"

"I'm not sure. I just know I'd like to get out of here in a hurry."

Robert nodded his head. "That's right, you've been gone."

"What's going on?"

"The same thing started happening to me and a number of others when Tom started using this lemon-scented disinfectant. My guess is it's some sort of chemical reaction. It clears up real quick."

Doug shook his head again. "Yeah, it's gone now."

The two men finished unloading the truck. Doug climbed into the front seat, retrieved his clipboard, and then headed for Mother Francesca's office.

As Doug approached the office, he passed Tom leaning on his broom. "Morning," said Tom.

"I hear it's going to be a fine one, too," Doug replied. "Not one cloud in the whole sky, and we're supposed to hit sixty-two degrees."

"I think the sidewalks are going to need sweeping today," he returned with a smile.

"Is Mother Francesca in yct?"

"She got in around six o'clock." He looked down the hall. "There she is."

Doug gave Tom a pat on his shoulder and began walking toward Mother Francesca. As he walked further and further into the nursing home, he felt his heart begin to pound again and the unwelcome feeling return.

"Finished already?" she asked.

"Robert helped."

She turned and motioned for him to follow her. "I left my pen on my desk."

They walked past the main entrance to a room containing several small offices. His heart continued to pound, and the palms of his hands continued to sweat. He could not remember a time in his life when he had felt more uncomfortable. The temptation to turn and flee the building without securing a signature was quickly becoming the sole focus of his thoughts.

"Did I put that pen back in the drawer?" Mother Francesca searched diligently. "It was right here."

Doug sat down. "It's by that folder."

She took the pen in hand and signed the invoice. "And how is your family?"

"Doing well. My wife might be having another baby."

"What delightful news."

"She sees the doctor later in the week. It's been a while since we had a baby in the house, but I wouldn't mind another one; a boy this time."

Mother Francesca looked over the stacks of papers and folders neatly arranged on her desktop, then she turned toward a bookcase that lined one wall of the room. The Tranquil Garden Nursing Home had yet to enter into the computer age. Here, instead, it was files of papers. Filling the shelves were dozens of binders containing state ordinances, safety and fire codes, financial data, staff and medication schedules, and all other information vital to the day-to-day operations of Tranquil Garden.

She pulled a neatly labeled white binder from the shelf and opened it. She held out her pen and asked, "If you will sign line six?" Doug looked up at her but said nothing. "Line six right there." Mother Francesca looked at him curiously. "Are you ill?"

"I've got a case of the jitters or something."

Mother Francesca sat down. "You are frightened?"

He wiped his sweating palms on his pants. "I'm not sure; I think so."

She lifted her hands into the air. "What could be frightening about a building full of old women?"

He forced a smile. "Nothing, I guess."

"Anything frightening about me?"

He looked into her eyes. "Nothing at all."

"A little fresh air, and you will be fine." She watched Doug sign his name in the binder. "We will see you on Wednesday."

"Actually, Thursday." He searched the pocket of his company-provided workshirt. "They changed the delivery schedule. Just give this number a call, and the people in the office can answer any questions. Robert said this would mess up your ordering information."

"Sister Mary Margaret enjoys a good challenge." Mother Francesca smiled at Doug as he stood up. "No more jitters?"

He shook his head. "Not a one."

Nine

Concluding her weekly reading to Abigail and Clare, Sister Janice said, "Before I go, I need to have a word with you, Sister Abigail."

Clare stood up. "If you will excuse me."

"There's no need for you to leave," Abigail said. "Sister Janice may say whatever she needs to say in your presence."

"I didn't mean to make it sound like that, Sister Clare. I am only bringing news."

"I could use some good news," Abigail said.

Sister Janice waited for Clare to sit back down. "Disappointing news, I am afraid. Sister Alicia has postponed her trip to come see you once again."

"And what reason did she give this time?"

"She has fallen ill, Sister. She underwent surgery this morning. Apparently her appendix burst without warning. I was told she is quite ill. I have placed her name on the intercessory list in the sanctuary."

"Thank you. Will they be sending another Sister in her place?"

"My understanding is they will not. Sister Alicia will be sent after she recuperates. I know you are disappointed, but the days will pass quickly."

Abigail nodded. "The Lord knows best."

Sister Janice took the old woman's hand and gave it a gentle squeeze. "Before you know it, you and Sister Alicia will be in the visitors' lounge, and you won't have a single memory of all this waiting."

"Thank you for bringing me the news."

She let go of Abigail's hand and walked toward the door. "Good day, Sisters."

Abigail waited until the scurrying sounds of youthful feet had faded. "Sister Janice was lying to me."

"Yes, she was," Clare agreed.

"With each passing day I am more cut off from my community. When I ask permission to call my convent, I am told the lines are down from blizzards. When I ask why I am not receiving any letters, I am told the mail has been delayed from the same blizzards." She made her way over to the night table and searched through the drawer. "Clare, have you taken anything out of this drawer?"

"No, I haven't."

"My letters—my letters from my community are gone."

Clare got out of her chair. "Are you sure? Could you have put them somewhere else?"

Abigail closed the drawer. "They are gone. Now I can't go to anyone with my concerns. I have no proof that a visit was ever to take place." She sat on the bed. "You read the letter to me. Was she coming or have I taken leave of my senses?"

"Your senses remain sharp, Abigail."

"I was supposed to have a visit. And she was going to relate to me the final prophecy of Sister Catherine."

Clare nodded. "She was."

"Sister Abigail?" a worried Sister Kathleen called from the hallway. She stepped into the room. "There you are. We thought you were down with a stroke or something."

"You are always waiting for us at the door when we come to make rosaries," Monica said.

"Forgive me," Abigail apologized as she used Clare's arm to help her get up from the bed. "I am well and eager to make rosaries with you this afternoon. Shall we go into the work-room?"

The nuns went to their stations silently. As Sister Kathleen distributed the supplies and Graciella passed out the pliers, Patrice said, "I heard George is coming to Tranquil Garden one week from tomorrow."

"Who is George?" Clare asked.

"He is a musician who comes every month or so," replied Monica. "He plays the most delightful music on his guitar. He wears his hair like a woman pulled up in a ponytail. I've never seen such a thing."

"I certainly have," Sister Kathleen announced. "Back in the seventies, my convent was located right across the street from one of those hippie outposts. That place was full of long-haired young people in their funny clothes. The only way you could tell the men from the women was by their beards."

"What were the hippies like?" Clare asked.

"They were the best neighbors we ever had. Those boys were always so helpful and so happy. It was all I could do most days to keep from chasing one of them down and giving him a haircut, but I never saw a bunch of happier young people."

Abigail nodded. "We had a group come through our property once. It was in the fall when the grounds were thickly covered with apples. The novices who were outside harvesting the apples caught sight of them and fled into the convent, leaving their baskets behind."

"They did look like a dangerous sort," Sister Kathleen said.

"Indeed, but just as in your case, we found them to be very friendly. Instead of trying to steal apples, as we thought, they had seen the novices gathering them and thought they would help out."

"I never saw a bunch of happier young people," Sister Kathleen repeated.

"Abigail?" Patrice said. "Let's get back to the story you were telling us. You left us with Sister Theresa heading down a spiritually perilous and corrupt path."

Abigail clipped off a piece of wire. "As I said last week, the powerful gift given to Sister Theresa was a dangerous one, and once she fed off of the tree of evil, she was quickly lost in the darkness she had chosen. It was becoming a growing suspicion to the others in The Order that Sister Theresa may have turned from the light of her Lord."

"So they removed Sister Theresa," Sister Kathleen said. She looked at Abigail over her glasses. "Didn't they?"

"The Superior General prayed and waited," Abigail answered. "There was nothing else for her to do because she lacked some crucial information. About that time, strange things began happening around the convent."

Monica lowered her pliers. "What kind of things?"

"Novices began turning up dead." The sounds of rustling beads stopped. "At first there were no witnesses to anything. It seemed only a series of tragic coincidences. But the Mistress of Novices came to firmly believe the accidents wouldn't stop until Novice Rachel was destroyed."

"Why Rachel?" Patrice asked.

Abigail took hold of a blue bead. "Her

rightful place was in The Order—and the powers of darkness, which were growing ever stronger in Sister Theresa, were determined to keep Rachel from ever taking that place. When used for evil, Sister Theresa's gift was capable of bending the will of the weak in faith to acts of darkness. Her lust to have souls drawn to her and not to our Lord was so intoxicating that she continued on the disastrous path. She was deceived into believing that she held the control, when in fact darkness began to rule her every thought. Her gift became a tool of murder. Her influence was so great that the few under her influence even assisted in ending the lives of the remaining novices. She did not have to manipulate or coerce, Sisters, she merely had to think.

"And no one could prove anything. One sister fell from a third-story window as she leaned outside to clean it. Another suddenly tripped while walking down the road, falling into the path of a speeding car. Another apparently fell asleep while resting in a warm bath and drowned, and there were others.

"Of course, nothing could be proven. At first there were no witnesses to anything, but several of the novices had very noticeable attachments to Sister Theresa, and one or more of them always seemed to be at or near the scenes of these deaths. Still, nothing could be proven. Those particular novices had such meek, loving natures that it seemed it had to be only a series of tragic coincidences."

"Why didn't Sister Theresa have just Novice Rachel killed?" Sister Kathleen asked.

"Good question," Patrice added. "Abigail?"

"Sister Theresa knew that one of the novices was rightly of The Order—but exactly which novice it was, eluded her knowledge. But the Mistress of Novices knew, and again she was faced with a choice. She could go to the Superior General, confess her misdeed so that Sister Theresa would be removed, and name Rachel as the true member of The Order. Or, she could continue to allow her pride to rule her actions."

"What did she do?" Monica asked. "Oh, I don't know if I want you to answer that."

"Go ahead and tell us," Sister Kathleen insisted.

"She chose the way of pride once again, I am afraid. She convinced herself that if she confessed her mistake, she would not be believed when she proclaimed that Rachel was truly the one to be placed in The Order."

Patrice slapped the tabletop. "You are telling us that the Mistress of Novices sat back and watched while Sister Theresa annihilated an entire class of novices?"

"No, she short-circuited the killings by declaring that each of the novices was unsuited to continue the religious training of the Sisters of the Divine Name. She dismissed the entire class."

"She canceled vocations?" Sister Kathleen asked. "I certainly wouldn't want to answer to God for that one."

Abigail began putting her work away. "The Mistress of Novices made arrangements for the remaining novices to go to other communities if they so chose, and she arranged transportation for those who decided to return to their families in order to have more time to discern their vocation."

"Didn't someone question what she was doing?" Patrice asked. "We are talking about an entire class of novices."

"Her position was a powerful one. Often she would determine that novices were unsuited to our way of life, and although an entire class had never been canceled before, no questions were raised. The entire matter of relocating the remaining twenty-four novices took only a few days to complete, and life continued on." Abigail turned toward Clare. "What time is it, dear?"

Clare looked at the clock. "You have twenty minutes."

"And I will need each one to get these weary legs to the chapel in time for my devotion."

Sister Kathleen groaned with displeasure. "Now wait a minute. You can't leave without telling us what happened to Sister Theresa."

Patrice asked, "Did she start killing off the professed Sisters next?"

"Don't even think such a thing." Monica looked up to Abigail. "Please say she didn't."

"If someone will help me up from my chair, I will conclude today's portion of the story."

Clare got up. "Here, take my hand."

Abigail looked out at the blurred figures sitting around the table. "Determined to seek revenge at any cost, Sister Theresa became a puppet to the forces of evil. Their aim was to bring the existence of The Order to a close by using any means available to them. And now, because the Mistress of Novices chose the way of pride, the Superior General was still unaware that she was dealing with anything other than a wayward nun in need of repentance."

Ten

Clare stood at the bathroom sink brushing her teeth. She heard someone tapping on the door. "I'm almost finished, Abigail," she said. After she had rinsed her mouth, she came out. "Are you ready for breakfast?"

"I am especially looking forward to this meal. This is Thursday, and Thursday means a fat cinnamon bun swimming in butter to go with my oatmeal."

The two made the journey to the dining room. When they reached the entrance, Clare stopped suddenly.

"We can't very well eat out here, child," Abigail said.

"You go on ahead," Clare suggested. "I will be along shortly. Can you manage?"

"Indeed I can." Abigail let go of Clare's arm and continued into the dining room.

Clare turned and went back along the same route she had just taken, but as she approached room 142, she did not slow her pace.

She continued to a door at the end of the hall and turned the gold-plated knob.

The door closed with a loud clang. Clare looked up at the steep flight of stairs to her right, then her gaze lowered to an elderly nun lying face down on the hard tile floor. She placed her hand on the woman's shoulder and soothingly called, "Florence—Florence."

"Clare!" she responded. "I can't . . . I can't move."

"I'll get help."

"It's too late. I'm all broken up inside."

"Oh, Florence."

"Stay with me."

"I'm here." Clare sat on the cold floor beside the injured woman. "I'm right here."

"I knew you would come." She took a shallow breath. "It hurts to breathe."

"Don't try to talk."

"But I must. You must know—I didn't fall. Someone pushed me."

"Are you sure?"

"Yes."

"Who, Florence? Who did this?"

"I—I don't know."

"It's all right," she soothed. "Rest easy. It won't be long."

"I tried to see you. They kept turning me back."

"Rest easy now."

"They wouldn't even let me eat in the dining room. Why wouldn't they let me be with you and Gloria?"

"It doesn't matter now."

"No."

"Be at peace, Florence."

"It hurts."

"I know."

"Tell me the story . . . of the girl who went to heaven."

Clare stroked the top of Florence's head. "She arrived in the morning, eager to explore God's kingdom. She ran out into the Field of Surrender, an open stretch of land with blades of pale green grass that were short, as if freshly mowed. She wondered, *Why are the blades of grass so pale?* The answer came, *Because you still cling to the riches of the earth.* She wondered again, *Why are the blades of grass so short?* The answer came, *Because you still cling to those who live on the earth.* 'Then I shall cling no more,' the child said. And with her words, the silver clouds released a gentle rain. Before her eyes the blades of grass deepened in color and grew in height, transforming into a brilliant meadow that led her to the arms of God."

"He is ever faithful," Florence said weakly. "Even now."

"Yes," agreed Clare. "He is."

"Are you all right?" Nurse Gertie asked as she bent over Clare in the stairwell. "Bless your heart. Sister Clare, can you hear me?"

"Yes—yes—I can hear you."

"You fainted," she explained. "You must have fallen. Sister Josephine heard the *thud*, and then we came in. It must have given you quite a start to find Florence that way. We need to get you back your room so they can move her. Can you get up?"

"I think so—will you help me?"

"Of course," she said quickly. "Here we go, nice and easy. Should I get you a wheelchair?"

"No, I'll be fine once I get up."

"I don't think you should try to walk."

"I'm all right."

Nurse Gertie wrapped her arm around the petite nun. "Let's get you back to your room, then I'll send a doctor in to make sure you didn't hurt yourself." As they made their way to the room, Nurse Gertie asked, "What were you doing in there? You should have been in the dining room."

"The Lord summoned me."

"Did He? Well, that wasn't the explanation I was expecting, but it will do. That back stairwell is almost never used, so I'm grateful

He did. We would have been looking all over for the poor woman thinking she had wandered off. The thought of how long she could have lain there—it's just awful."

They came to room 142. "Is that you, Nurse Gertie?" Abigail asked.

"Sister Clare has had a bit of a jolt."

"I'm all right, Abigail."

"She found Sister Florence at the bottom of the stairwell and fainted."

"Have her lie down," Abigail said firmly. "Here, this one is her bed."

"I don't need to lie down," Clare insisted. "There is nothing wrong with me."

Nurse Gertie turned toward Abigail. "Have her stay put until I come back with my equipment. I want to check her blood pressure and listen to her heart."

"I will," Abigail promised. "Sister Florence, is she all right?"

"She is in the Lord's eternal embrace," answered Clare.

"Keep her in bed," Nurse Gertie said as she started for the door. "I'll be right back."

"I don't need to be in bed," Clare protested. "I feel fine."

"You will stay right where you are," insisted Abigail.

"There is nothing wrong with me."

"Then it would be reasonable to assume that your visit to Florence was another of your holy excursions. And it would be reasonable to assume that your physical state when Nurse Gertie found you was not the result of fainting." Clare remained silent. "You were given a glimpse into the inner world of the kingdom."

"Are you prying into my affairs?"

"Yes."

"And that is my answer as well."

Wheeling the medical equipment cart into the room, Nurse Gertie said, "Let me check your blood pressure, Sister Clare. Your heart rate must still be over 100 after a shock like that."

Clare sat up. "This really isn't necessary."

"You let me decide that." She wrapped the blood pressure cuff around Clare's arm. "Are you having any chest pains?"

"No."

"Shortness of breath?"

"No."

Mother Francesca came into the room. "I was told that Sister Clare fainted? Is she all right?"

"Her blood pressure is normal, so is her pulse, but she was really out of it in the stairwell."

"Can you get her to the infirmary, or shall I have the doctor come in and examine her?"

"Please," said Clare, "that won't be necessary. I'm fine."

Nurse Gertie shook her head. "She's had

quite a shock. I don't think we should move her."

"Then I will send for the doctor at once." Mother Francesca went to the door and then turned. "Keep her still until she has been evaluated. Let me know what his findings are."

Clare gave a heavy sigh.

"What's the long face for?" Nurse Gertie asked.

"No one is listening to me."

"Of course we are."

"I told you I was fine."

"This won't take more than a minute or two. You just relax and let us take care of you."

Eleven

The dining room of the Tranquil Garden Nursing Home buzzed with numerous voices speaking at the same time. It was the lunch hour, and although there could have been many topics of conversation taking place at each of the tables, there was only one: the death of Sister Florence.

"Pass me the salt, Sister Abigail," Sister Kathleen asked.

"That isn't salt," Patrice said.

Sister Kathleen turned toward her. "Then what is it?"

"Salt substitute."

"But I want salt."

"I don't think they have it." Patrice pushed the saltshaker forward. "Go on and use it. If I hadn't said anything you never would have known."

"No thank you. I've been putting salt, real salt, on my food since I was old enough to hold the shaker. I'd rather do without."

"Patrice," Monica said. "Finish telling us what Nurse Gertie told you about Sister Florence."

"It is just horrible. Everyone thinks Florence was pushed down the stairs. Nurse Gertie said they found four long, thin bruises on her upper arm. The size and spacing suggest the bruising was made by someone's hand."

"You mean Sister Florence didn't fall?" Sister Kathleen asked. "It wasn't an accident?"

Monica closed her eyes. "That can't be true."

Abigail secured a forkful of green beans. "She was new to us, wasn't she?"

"She was from my community," Clare answered. "We arrived on the same day."

"Florence was the one you had so much trouble locating," said Abigail.

"The one I never located until yesterday."

"I wasn't finished," Patrice continued. "Doug, the young man who makes the food deliveries, was seen going into the stairwell on the second floor just after six o'clock in the morning." Patrice wiped her mouth with her napkin. "In all of my years here, Doug has made his deliveries on Mondays and Fridays, but he was seen here by several people on Thursday morning."

Sister Kathleen lifted her glass of water. "I want to know why he would be up there."

"Who saw him on the second floor?" Abigail asked.

"Her name slips my mind," Patrice answered. "It was—it was—Eunice."

"Sister Eunice has been off the mark for years," Sister Kathleen stated. "She sees Tom every other morning mopping the roof tiles, and we all know Tom has never been up on that roof. I wouldn't take that remark too seriously."

"She knows what she saw," Patrice argued.

Sister Kathleen pointed toward the ceiling. "She's a second-floor resident, isn't she?"

Patrice put down her napkin. "What does that have to do with anything?"

"They put people up there for a reason, and we all know what that is."

"That doesn't mean Eunice didn't see him."

"And it doesn't dismiss the bruising on Florence's arm," Abigail said.

"Why would anyone want to kill her?" Monica asked. "Clare, she was from your community. What type of work did she do?"

"She worked in hospitals and nursing homes. She made visits and did simple acts of kindness."

"Hard to make enemies under those circumstances," Sister Kathleen said. "Was she hard to get along with?"

"Not at all. She had a very considerate nature."

Monica straightened in her chair. "Maybe it was just an accident. Maybe she fainted or something."

Sister Kathleen pointed her fork toward the center of the table. "Then how did she get those bruises?"

"If I may have your attention," said Mother Francesca with a loud voice. "Sisters, if I may please have your attention." The room grew quiet. "I know there is much alarm and concern over the death last week of one of our residents. I would like to take a few moments to clarify the situation for you, and answer any questions that may linger.

"Shall we begin with prayer?" She looked across the room. "Sister Janice, if you will lead us."

Sister Janice left the place by the wall where she was standing and stood beside Mother Francesca. She paused briefly while all heads in the room bowed. "Merciful Father, may our hearts be opened for the truth to be heard so that all speculation may end. Comfort those who were touched by the life of Sister Florence, and bring them Your peace. Amen."

Mother Francesca put her hands into her pockets. "Thank you, Sister Janice. We have the preliminary medical results concerning Sister Florence. The official cause of death has been issued to be heart failure brought on by injuries sustained in the fall she had from the second-floor staircase. What caused the fall remains unclear at this time."

Mother Francesca waited for the reaction in the room to ease. "As for the bruising to the arm of Sister Florence, which seems to have fueled much of the speculation that foul play was involved—that was caused by one of our staff the day prior to the accident. As each of you knows, our bodies are much more delicate in our advanced years. On the day before the accident, Sister Janice was in Sister Florence's room, concluding a devotional reading for her. It was the practice of Sister Florence to escort Sister Janice to the door, and on this occasion she became lightheaded. Sister Janice reacted instinctively, clutching her arm to prevent a fall."

She looked about the room. "We all know the childlike gentleness of Sister Janice. There is no abuse here, Sisters." She paused for a moment to allow the information to be absorbed. "Are there any questions?"

A nun up in the front asked, "Mother, what about the delivery man who was seen on the second floor?"

"Yes, Mother," the nun beside her said. "The young man was here on a Thursday, and in the six years that I have been here, he has never come on a Thursday."

Mother Francesca lifted her hands high to

silence a new round of murmuring. "I believe the man you are referring to is Doug Brennan, and he was here the morning Florence was found. Our food distributor changed our delivery day from Fridays to Thursdays. Sister Mary Margaret labored several hours preparing for this change, and I can assure you that Doug ventured no farther than my office door. I personally escorted him back to the kitchen after signing his invoice, and I personally watched from the landing as his truck pulled away." She looked around the room again.

"Any other questions?" She waited silently for a moment. "Please, Sisters—continue your meal."

The dining room filled with the sounds of silverware clinking and conversations resuming.

"I wonder what Florence was doing in that stairwell in the first place," Patrice said. "It wasn't anywhere near her room."

Monica placed her hands on the sides of her face. "Don't stir it all up again. Oh, I think this is giving me a headache."

"There you are, Abigail," a nun in a black habit said.

"That is the voice of Emily," Abigail said. "Emily, is that you?"

"It is."

"Sit! Sit!" she invited. "When did you arrive?"

"This morning," she answered as she pulled up another chair to the crowded table.

"You must be exhausted." Abigail reached for her hand. "Which room are you in?"

"No room for me this time, Abigail, I'm strictly a visitor. I will only be here for a couple of days, then it's back to upstate New York for me."

"I hear they had a terrible snowstorm."

A confused expression appeared on Emily's face. "Not that I know of. We've actually had one of the mildest winters that I can remember."

"Then I must be mistaken." Abigail pointed across the table. "Emily, you remember Patrice, Monica, Graciella, and Sister Kathleen."

Emily nodded to each of them. "Yes, of course. What a delight to see you again."

"And beside me here is Clare. She is new to Tranquil Garden this year. Clare, this is Emily, who was with us last year while recuperating from a bout of pleurisy."

Emily focused her large black eyes on Clare for a moment. "Do I know you?"

"I thought the same thing when I met her," Abigail confessed. "She is a Sister of the Sacred Heart."

"Hmm. I am afraid I never heard of them."

"We were a small community."

"If it comes to you, Emily, don't reveal the location," said Abigail. "I've been guessing since her arrival." She put her fork down. "I know, it was Father John's retreat on Scripture meditation in Cleveland, 1948."

"I've never been to Cleveland."

"Emily," said Monica, "where are you staying?"

"With the Sisters of Mercy right up the street," she answered. "Sister Janice wouldn't hear of my staying in a hotel. She insisted that I stay with them."

Abigail leaned toward Emily. "When you return to the Northeast, would you do me the greatest favor and inquire at my convent about something?"

"It would be a delight, Abigail. What would you like me to inquire about?"

"I am not receiving any letters from my community, and I would like you to remind the sisters that I rely heavily on the companionship I receive from those letters."

"I will stop by the Motherhouse personally and get to the bottom of it."

"That is too far out of your way. I couldn't ask such a favor."

"I can't pass up an opportunity to see the Motherhouse or the Sisters."

"You've been to Abigail's convent before?" Patrice asked.

Emily smiled. "I spent nearly a year there as a novice."

Sister Kathleen's eyes widened. "Then you

must have been there when Sister Theresa went into The Order."

"Actually, I was."

Sister Kathleen nudged Abigail. "She wasn't one of the novices that—that helped out with the accidents?"

Abigail laughed. "She was not."

"You told them about the history of The Order?" Emily asked with surprise.

"I haven't finished the story, so say no more. Sisters, you are indeed speaking with one who was a novice during the time of Sister Theresa."

"Did you know Novice Rachel?" Monica asked.

"I did," she answered. "We often studied together."

Monica moved her chair closer. "What was she like?"

"She was like any other Sister. I don't remember a great deal about her. Our class was together less than a year, but I recall that Rachel was very—ordinary. When Abigail told me the story last year, I was surprised. I never would have guessed that she was being considered for entry into The Order."

Patrice pulled her napkin from her collar. "You mean you didn't know what was going on with Sister Theresa and Sister Rachel?"

"I was a young novice concerned with discovering whether I had found the community where the Lord intended for me to serve out my vocation. We knew Sister Theresa went into The Order, but none of us knew that a mistake had been made."

"A deadly mistake," Abigail said with a sigh. "The Mistress of Novices made a choice based on appearances."

"A choice anyone would have made who had witnessed roomfuls of nuns falling by the wayside as the Holy Spirit swept over them." Emily caressed Abigail's hand as she spoke. "The Mistress of Novices could not have foreseen the turn Sister Theresa would make or the path she would insist on following."

Monica stirred sugar into her coffee. "Tell us more about Rachel."

"Time is amazing. It can wipe away so many things. It was weeks before I recognized Abigail when I stayed here last year."

"Had Sister Danielle not involved our entire table in a conversation concerning our communities I doubt it would have happened at all," Abigail said. "But it wasn't her gray hair or her wrinkled skin, which I can no longer see, that kept her disguised from me: Emily once had a profound Southern accent."

"Fifty-five years of living in Chicago took care of that." Emily turned her head upward and laughed without warning. "I do remember something about Rachel—something positively non-angelic."

"What was that?" Patrice asked with interest.

"Don't tell us," Monica protested. "Abigail, isn't this gossip?"

"It isn't gossip," Sister Kathleen said firmly. "Go ahead, Sister Emily."

"She could not sing to save her life. She absolutely could not find her way through the simplest melody line. It was a terrible thorn for her because she truly loved music, and it was a terrible thorn for our ears as we listened to her attempts."

"It was penance for all of us," Abigail added. "But out of obedience she had to sing when told to sing." She laughed, and the others joined her. "There were many in our community who were certainly not singers, myself included, but she truly had a profound lacking."

Emily looked at Monica. "At what point are you in the story?"

"Don't get them started," Abigail warned. "The story is told only during our weekly meetings to make rosaries."

Patrice pushed her plate aside. "We are at the part where the Mistress of Novices shipped out the entire class of novices."

Emily nodded. "Have you told them what happened to Sister Theresa?"

"No, not yet."

"I would have burned her at the stake," Sister Kathleen said.

"I don't know, there are worse things than an agonizing death," Emily said. "Like spending a lifetime living with the choices you've made."

Twelve

It was a warm, cloudless Sunday afternoon. With slow steps Abigail walked toward the visiting area near the main entrance of Tranquil Garden.

"Abigail!" Emily called. She came over and took Abigail's arm. "I'm with Sister Mary Lawrence. Let me lead you to a chair."

"Good afternoon, Sister Mary Lawrence." Abigail waited for a response. "GOOD AFTERNOON, SISTER," she said a little louder.

"And good afternoon to you, Sister."

"Are you ready for your flight, Emily?" Abigail asked.

"THE TAXI SHOULD BE HERE SOON," she answered loudly. "THANK YOU BOTH FOR SEEING ME OFF." Her voice quieted. "Abigail, while I was enjoying a time of recreation with the Sisters of Mercy yesterday evening, I spoke with Sister Janice about your letters. She confessed to me that she has been lying to you."

"What did she lie about?"

"You haven't been receiving any letters, none at all. She told you something about snow-storms, I believe, but in truth she just didn't want you to feel abandoned."

"And she felt lying was the proper way to protect my feelings?" Abigail sighed. "Sister Janice is indeed young."

"I thought you would prefer the truth, but I'm not really sure that is the truth."

"I hear concern in your voice."

"Last night was so strange. I can't tell you how I knew, but I felt certain that Sister Janice was lying also to me. I decided to see Mother Francesca and discuss the matter with her."

"And what did she say?"

"She never said anything. I was told she had taken ill and had gone on to bed, but, again, I felt certain that was not the truth. I was left wondering if Mother Francesca ever knew of my request to speak to her. I think something is wrong here."

"A feeling that has been growing in my heart as well—"

"Emily," Sister Mary Lawrence inter-rupted, "I will miss you."

Emily leaned over and kissed the woman's cheek. "I plan to be back in time for your birth-day this summer."

Sister Mary Lawrence gave her a blank look. "What?"

"I WILL BE BACK IN JUNE—FOR YOUR BIRTHDAY."

The nun's face lit up as if she had just opened some wonderful gift. "In June then."

Emily turned back to Abigail. "I hesitate in leaving you here."

"Great good always attracts great evil. With so many dedicated souls under one roof it is to be expected."

"I understand, but I feel this is different."

"It may be, but I can assure you that it has no interest in me. Don't let your trip be weighted with concerns."

"Your taxi is here," Sister Josephine said. "It's time to leave for the airport."

"Is that you, Sister Josephine?"

"Yes, Abigail, it is. Now say good-bye to Sister Emily. She must be on her way."

"Could I come outside to see her off?"

Sister Josephine gave her approval and left the nuns to walk at their slower pace. As they neared the entrance, Emily noticed Sister Josephine talking to the cab driver.

"Take your time, Sisters," Sister Josephine said as she walked back past them. "The driver took me up on an invitation for a cup of coffee."

"What a glorious day," Emily said. "I love to fly on days like this. The views are breathtaking."

"How I would like to be with you on that

plane on my way back to the Motherhouse," said Abigail.

"Things will seem better tomorrow. The sisters will straighten everything out, and you will be back in full communication."

"Tomorrow seems a year away." She smiled. "But I know it isn't. I will pray for patience as you complete the journey."

"Perhaps it is nothing more than a mix-up. Maybe they put a novice in charge of the mail, and she has decided that the effort of addressing and stamping letters is only necessary once a month."

"You will call me when you have word?"

"I will."

"One fresh cup of coffee with two sugars," Sister Josephine said as she came out the entrance. She took the cup to the driver's window and handed it to him. "Emily, time to go."

Sister Josephine stepped back to the curb. "Abigail, she's waving to you." The elderly nun raised her hand and began to wave. The taxi followed the driveway around the fountain and out to the main road. "You can stop waving, Abigail. They are gone now."

"May I stay outside? I would like to go to the fountain on this beautiful afternoon, even if only for a moment."

"Let me help you across the driveway."

"Thank you, Sister."

They began to walk toward the fountain.

"I have a couple of things to do, then I will return and bring you back." She led Abigail to the cement ledge of the fountain. "It's just past two o'clock. I should be back by a quarter after. I hope that's enough time."

"I am grateful for it. You have been an angel of mercy to one of our Lord's least ones."

"Now, I want you to stay at the fountain until I get back. Don't try to cross the driveway by yourself."

"I promise I will stay right here."

Sister Josephine left Abigail to enjoy the sound of the falling water. She reached toward the water. The mild air and abundant sunshine had been deceiving. She pulled her hand back quickly as the sudden chill jolted her entire body.

A moment passed. The tranquil sounds of the water were interrupted by the muffled cries of someone on the other side of the fountain. It took Abigail several minutes to decide exactly where the soft sobs were originating from. Then with a heart filled with concern, Abigail moved slowly toward the sound until she caught a glimpse of a blurred figure sitting on the cement ledge.

"Is something wrong, child?"

A round-shouldered woman with deep brown hair turned her head. "Thank you for asking, Abigail."

"Nurse Dorothy? Is that you?"

"It's me."

"Why are you crying?"

"I've lost my job," she sobbed.

"You lost your job?" Abigail repeated.

Nurse Dorothy wiped her eyes with a wet tissue. "I was fired, Abigail. I no longer work here. I pick up my final paycheck today."

"I don't understand. You are a wonderful nurse."

"I was Sister Florence's nurse, and they— it turned into a big mess." She blew her nose. "No one will believe me. Not even Mother Francesca."

"Tell me and I will believe you."

She wiped her eyes again. "The usual night nurse got sick so I was called in early to finish the night shift. I made a quick check of the rooms when I came on duty. Florence wasn't in her bed, and she wasn't in the hallway, so I called over to the convent. Sister Janice told me not to worry, Florence had become ill and was down in Critical Care. But then, after they found Florence, she swore she never said such a thing. She said I failed to keep track of my patients. She thinks the accident was my fault. It wasn't."

"Of course not," Abigail soothed. "And it doesn't matter what she thinks. God knows, and He believes you."

"You believe me."

"I do." The woman began to cry again. "It's all right," Abigail assured her. "You will go on to a place more worthy of your service."

"I don't want to leave. I love my patients."

"You can continue to love your patients wherever the Lord sends you. No one can stop you from loving." Abigail motioned toward the front of Tranquil Garden. "And this is only a place, nothing more. Leave it here, and go where the Lord leads you."

"Thank you, Abigail," said Nurse Dorothy as she dried her eyes one more time. "I feel much better."

"Then may I ask your help in a difficulty I am having?"

"Anything, Sister."

"I am wondering where I can get an out-of-state phone book."

"If you're trying to find a phone number, it would be easier to call information. All you have to do is dial 4-1-1. Then they'll take it from there and put you in touch with the national directory. It's much easier than a phone book."

"Of course!" Abigail smiled. "The thought didn't cross my mind. Thank you, child."

Nurse Dorothy stood up and straightened her clothes. "I better go in."

"You sound as though you were marching to your doom. This is not an ending, it is a beginning. Our Lord has already picked out a new place for you to work, and He will lead you to it." Abigail waved to the woman. "When word comes, write to me and share your good news."

Thirteen

With a small paperback book under her arm, Sister Janice walked toward room 142. She had a noticeable spring in her step, an excitement beyond her usual youthful eagerness.

"Am I intruding?"

"We are recuperating from that delicious supper in the dining room," Abigail answered. "I don't think I will be able to move for at least another hour. How we got from the dining room into here is no less a miracle than the parting of the Red Sea."

"We are certainly going to miss your humor around here when you leave us again." Sister Janice walked over to the sitting area. "I have wonderful news! I am so excited that I don't think I will ever get to sleep tonight. I am being trained for a top administrative position by Mother Francesca herself—the only higher position in the community is Superior General!"

"Congratulations," said Clare.

"That's why I'm here, Sisters. I will be in Houston for a few days and won't be able to come tomorrow for your reading. I thought that instead of waiting until next week, I would go ahead and read to you this evening." She displayed a book and said, "Sister Kathleen gave me *A Compilation of the Writings of the Desert Fathers*. She said she thought you both would enjoy it."

"She has an ability to select the most profound readings," Abigail said. "This will indeed be a treat."

The young woman sat down and began reading.

Between a full stomach and the gentle tone of Sister Janice's voice, Abigail found herself battling to stay awake. After thirty minutes she could fight it no more.

"Sister Abigail is asleep," Sister Janice said in a whisper. A loud snore came from the old woman. "She must really be tired. Should we help her to the bed?"

"I will see to it later."

Sister Janice closed the book and got up. "Then I'll be on my way," she said quietly.

"Thank you for the reading. And good luck to you in Houston."

"Why is everyone whispering?" Abigail asked.

"We didn't want to wake you," Clare answered.

"Are you leaving us, Sister Janice?"

"I'm due in room 163 shortly, but I'm glad you are awake. Earlier, I intended to tell you how sorry I was . . . I guess with all the excitement of my trip, it slipped my mind. I am so sorry about your friend Sister Emily."

"I have received no news about her."

"Didn't someone from our staff tell you about the accident?"

"No."

"We received a call about Sister Emily. The accident—it happened on the way to the airport. They think the driver suffered a heart attack behind the wheel."

"Was the accident a bad one?"

"She will be fine. Please don't worry."

Anger flashed into Abigail's eyes. "I am not a child, Sister Janice. And I would prefer to know what her true condition is."

"It will only upset you."

"Then nothing will change, because I am already upset."

"All right," Sister Janice said softly. "She is alive, but her condition is very critical."

"May I go to her?"

"That would be out of the question. She's been flown to a trauma center in Houston where she can get the finest care. When we have further word, I will make sure that you receive it. Sister Mary Lawrence is holding an hour of intercession for her at eight o'clock."

"I will be there. Thank you for telling me."

Sister Janice palmed her book and left the room.

"It's nearing eight o'clock now," said Clare. "We should be on our way."

"First, I will need something. Would you go to the drawer of the night table and remove a piece of paper? I will need a pen too—please see if there is a pen as well." Abigail started toward the door. "Are you coming?"

Clare rushed to gather supplies. She caught up with Abigail. "Hold on to my arm."

Abigail wrapped her ancient hand around Clare's arm, just above the elbow. "Dear Emily. How I wish I could come to your side. Faster, child, we must move faster."

"We will be there before eight o'clock."

"Eight o'clock? What happens at eight o'clock?"

"The time of intercession that's being offered for Emily," Clare said patiently. "That's why we are going to the sanctuary."

"Oh yes—but first we must go to the dining room. I must make another call."

As they approached the adjoining hallway, Clare said, "Then I will take you to the dining room."

"I was hoping you would, as I wouldn't be able to read my own handwriting."

The women made their way down the hall,

slowly as always. Abigail limped slightly as a nagging touch of arthritis sent pain racing up one leg. The trip took them in the direction of an upside-down letter L, up one long hallway laced with lemon-scented disinfectant, followed by a shorter journey down the east/west hallway.

Abigail placed the receiver to her ear. "Get the paper and pen ready. How did you get the outside line?"

Clare pushed 9. "You should hear a dial tone."

"I do." She felt for the buttons. "Four, one, one," she said as she pressed each number. "There, it's ringing." She waited a moment. "Yes, dear, I need a number in Westbury, Massachusetts. Thank you." She lowered the receiver. "Where is your ear, child?"

"Over here," she said as she pulled the phone to her. Clare wrote a number down. "Take the phone again, Abigail. I'll dial the number." She cleared the line and placed the call. "It should be ringing."

"To whom am I speaking?"

"This is long-distance information."

"Very good. Hello? Yes—could you give me the number of the Sisters of the Divine Name convent on Plaffit Avenue? Thank you."

She put the phone to Clare's ear and waited until sounds of the pen marking the paper stopped.

"You can hang up, Abigail." Clare tore off the section of paper with the number on it. "I have the number to your convent right here."

"One more call, and my questions will find answers."

"Sister Abigail? Sister Clare?" Mother Francesca called. "What are you two doing in here?"

Clare placed her hands into the pockets of her habit as Abigail hung up the phone. "We are on our way to the sanctuary. They are having intercessions for Emily, who was in the accident this afternoon."

"I am aware of that," she said calmly. "I am also aware that this is not the sanctuary."

"No," Abigail said slowly. "It isn't."

"Then why are you in here using the phone?" Abigail remained silent. "You know all calls are to be made through Sister Janice so a record for billing can be kept. Who are you trying to call?"

"No one."

"Abigail, why are you being difficult?" Mother Francesca looked at Clare's pocket. "What is that?"

Clare looked down at the portion of white paper sticking out of her pocket. "It's a piece of paper."

"I can see that," Mother Francesca said patiently. "May I have a look at it?"

"Of course," Clare answered.

"Whose number is this?"

Abigail lowered her head. "It's the number to my convent."

"How grateful I am for a complete answer. Sister Janice has informed me about the communication problems we've been experiencing with your convent, but sneaking around isn't the way we do things, Sister Abigail. I am disappointed in you." She folded the piece of paper and put it into her own pocket. "You won't be needing this."

"But I need that number to call," Abigail protested.

"Sister Janice will be back in a few days, and when she returns I will have her resume efforts to reach your convent." She wrapped her arm around Abigail and said, "I am surprised that after all of your years in community life that you would try to avert our rules here at Tranquil Garden."

Abigail remained silent.

"I believe it is time for prayer to begin," Mother Francesca said. "Be on your way now."

Clare escorted Abigail to the door of the dining room. She turned her head to see Mother Francesca going out the back entrance. "She didn't get the number."

"But she took the paper."

"Let me show you." Clare reached into her pocket. She took out a piece of paper and handed it to Abigail. "I tore the paper in half before we were discovered. She got the number to the long-distance information operator. That is the number to your community."

Abigail fisted the smaller piece of paper. "To attempt this again would be direct disobedience, but . . . if I must, I must." She put the paper into her pocket. "I will not lead you into sin, child. If your conscience would allow it, however, I will need to have the number read to me until I have it committed to memory. I warn you now, I have no mind for numbers. It will be no small task, but one I must complete if the truth is to be revealed."

Fourteen

Monica took her seat at the workroom table. "Is everyone going to the activity room tomorrow to hear George play his guitar?" A chorus of affirmatives erupted. "Why don't we all sit together?"

"Sounds fine to me," Sister Kathleen said. "It's closer to our room, so Monica and I will probably get there first. We'll save the seats."

"Sorry I'm late," Patrice said as she came around the table. "After lunch I went to visit Sister Ida in the Critical Care Unit."

"What is she doing in there?" Sister Kathleen asked.

Patrice organized her supplies. "She's very ill, Sisters. I heard the nurses discussing her situation, and one of them is in big trouble."

"Why?" Clare asked.

"For years Sister Ida has had trouble swallowing her medications, so they have begun putting them in her coffee."

"They do that for Sister Gina too," Monica added.

"Yesterday, one of the nurses put her afternoon heart medication into a cup of decaf coffee for Sister Judith to take to her as she always does, but somehow Sister Ida got a cup of regular coffee with no medication in it."

"Is that why she's sick?" Monica asked.

Patrice nodded. "That medication has been keeping her alive for the last year. It is powerful stuff."

"So the nurse forgot to put in the medicine?" Sister Kathleen asked.

"She insists she dissolved the medicine in a cup at five minutes before two o'clock, and left it on the counter in the kitchen just as she has done every afternoon since Sister Ida was put on the medication."

"It couldn't have walked off by itself," Sister Kathleen said. "And if one of us got it by mistake we would sure know it. Some heart medicines can be deadly if you take them when you don't need them."

Monica looked up. "I wonder what happened to it?"

Abigail, who had been quiet the whole time, spoke up. "I think I know, Sisters," she said seriously. "Yesterday, about two o'clock, I was there when Sister Josephine brought a cup of coffee to Emily's taxi driver—who had a fatal heart attack soon after, on the way to the airport."

"The medicine was in his coffee?" said Monica.

"Wouldn't they have figured that out at the hospital?" Patrice asked.

Clare looked toward Abigail. "How old was the taxi driver?"

"As with everything else that passes before these eyes, all I saw was a blur. I couldn't begin to guess his age."

Patrice said, "If the man fit the standard heart attack profile there would be no reason to suspect anything further. If he were older and a bit overweight, or if he came in with the stench of tobacco smoke clinging to his clothes, that would be the end of any speculation."

"Abigail, you should inform Mother Francesca right away," Monica encouraged. "Many of us are dependent on our medications, and if there are any dangers in how they are being dispensed, I'm sure she would want to correct that immediately."

"I will do that," Abigail assured. "I think we should offer a prayer for the soul of the taxi driver, and for the recovery of Emily."

The sound of rustling beads stopped as heads bowed for prayer. After a long silence, one by one, the Sisters resumed their work.

Monica looked over to Abigail, watching as the ancient hands maneuvered the pliers with ease. Feeling a nudge, Monica turned. Sister Kathleen motioned toward Abigail.

Leaning toward Kathleen, Monica whispered, "What is it?"

"Ask her."

"Ask her what?" Patrice said loudly.

Sister Kathleen's face flushed. "Never mind, Sister."

Monica leaned toward her again. "I'm sorry," she whispered. "What do you want me to ask?"

"I can ask myself, thank you," she said quietly. Her eyes raised to Abigail. "Aren't you going to begin the story?"

"Oh, the story," Monica said. "Yes, Abigail, you promised to tell us what happened to Sister Theresa."

"And I shall. Let me see—had the novices been sent away from the community?"

"You stopped just after that," Monica said.

"Then I left you with the community in quite a state: a Mistress of Novices locked in the grip of pride, a nun appointed to The Order who was under the influence of the powers of darkness, and a Superior General who, like the rest of the community, was still unaware of what was actually wrong. The story continues as the Mistress of Novices reasons that exposing Sister Theresa is no longer an option she could afford to take without risking her own position, so she begins to wait."

"Wait for what?" Sister Kathleen asked. "For Sister Theresa to make friends among the professed and start up a new killing spree?"

"She waited for the Superior General, who

was already growing suspicious, to discover the allegiance with darkness Theresa had made and to resolve the situation."

"That way," Patrice interrupted, "it wouldn't look like the Mistress of Novices had made a mistake."

"That is absolutely right, Patrice. She believed Sister Theresa would be exposed and removed. Then at the next class of novices, one would come forward displaying the powerful spiritual gifts given to the others of The Order, and all would be restored."

"Did that happen?" Monica asked.

"I'm afraid the Mistress of Novices was in for a surprise. Sister Theresa had a temporary change of heart. For the next several months she donned sackcloth and ashes, and was the most model nun I have ever seen. But once another class of novices was formed, she was up to her old tricks again. She quickly gained influence over some of the young novices."

"Did accidents start happening again?" Monica asked.

"Luckily, the Superior General confronted Sister Theresa before another tragedy took place. Sister Theresa was told to leave The Order. She would be allowed to return to the community on the condition that she cease her improper activities, repent before God, and attend the next novitiate class."

"She went back to the novitiate?" Patrice asked.

"She refused to go anywhere. She barricaded herself for nearly a week in the prayer chamber reserved for those of The Order. The authorities finally had to be called, and Sister Theresa was taken to a mental asylum." Abigail shuddered. "I can still hear her screams coming from the prayer chamber as they were taking her out."

"How horrible for you, Abigail," Clare said.

"It was horrible for the entire community. I suspected early on that there was evil working in her, but to hear it manifest itself is a sound I shall never forget." She felt for another bead. "There were many who believed young Theresa was simply very ill. I also had my doubts until I went to the asylum. After seeing her, I knew with certainty that it was not illness. Like a bride, she had given herself to her callous mate, allowing him to sow seeds of darkness deep into her soul."

"How did you know?" Sister Kathleen asked.

"It was something she said to me on my last visit."

After waiting quietly, Sister Kathleen said, "You are going to tell us what she said?"

Abigail put her pliers down. "She said, 'The Order is over, Abigail.' The sound of the words seemed to raise her to some perverse level of ecstasy. It was a pitiful sight that thankfully lasted only a moment. Then she seemed as sweet and innocent as a schoolgirl. But I have never experienced such coldness, nor would I care to again. Her final words have continued to echo in my mind throughout the years: 'The Order will be no more.'"

"I would have jumped out of my skin getting out of there." Sister Kathleen shuddered. "I hoped she enjoyed her nice long stay at the asylum."

"Within a year, she was treated, cured, and released," Abigail said. "—At least, she convinced her doctors that she was cured."

"Did she come back to the Sisters of the Divine Name?" Monica asked with concern.

"She did not attempt re-admittance, but I am sure it would have been denied her in any case."

"After that lapse in the prayer chamber, I would think so," Sister Kathleen said. She looked at the clock on the wall. "Keep going, Abigail."

"Well, when the fall came around again, another class of novices had been admitted into the novitiate. The Mistress of Novices began her task of watching for the deeper workings of the Holy Spirit within those novices, fully expecting a replacement for Sister Theresa."

"A replacement never came," Graciella said.

"We were blessed with a class of young girls with sincere vocations to the community, but none of them were called to The Order. God had selected Novice Rachel and no other."

"So the Mistress of Novices finally did the right thing and told the Superior General about Novice Rachel," Sister Kathleen said.

"She did not." Abigail resumed her work. "She did nothing, and The Order carried on with eleven. The favor of the Holy Spirit remained on the group, blessing them with visions, prophecies, and powerful intercessory gifts.

"The Mistress of Novices convinced herself that all was well, and that the new member of The Order would be found in the next class of novices."

"Was she?" Monica asked.

Abigail shook her head. "Not in that class or in the two classes that followed. Then, in the following year another member of The Order became ill, and it became apparent that she would soon be reaching the end of her life. And again there were no deeper workings of the Holy Spirit among any of the novices."

The room became quiet.

"Why did you stop the story?" Patrice asked. She looked at the clock on the wall again. "It's not time to stop yet."

"The next segment is rather lengthy, Sisters. I think this is a good place to end the story."

"If you enjoy torturing us by leaving the story up in the air, it is a wonderful place to stop," Sister Kathleen said sharply. "But for the rest of us, I think stopping here is simply cruel."

"Very well, then, I will continue. My attempt to place a phone call can wait until later." She cleared her throat. "The Order became ten in number before the Mistress of Novices finally realized that Novice Rachel had to be found and restored to them." Abigail picked up a bead. "Without discussing the matter with the Superior General, she set out to find her, but several years already had passed since the dismissal of that first group of novices, and there was no trace of young Rachel. Her mother, who was her only living relative, died in the spring of the previous year. There was no one to contact, and there was nowhere for the Mistress of Novices to turn for information. Rachel could have joined another community or married, or simply moved across the country."

"She never found her," Monica said.

"She never did. The Mistress of Novices returned from her search to confess all to the Superior General. The remaining ten sisters gathered in the prayer chamber, and for three days the group fasted and prayed. On the third day one of the sisters was given a vision."

"Tell us the vision, Abigail," Monica said.

"The Sister saw white sand and a leaf that

was old, dried, and withered. Then another leaf appeared. This leaf was young and fresh and green. A second young leaf appeared, followed by more, until eleven young leaves formed a circle around the old, withered one."

"What did it mean?" Patrice asked.

"It was believed to mean that when The Order was one in member, and that member was old, then all would be restored."

Monica smiled. "How wonderful."

"Had it been a correct interpretation, it would have been," Abigail said. "Sister Catherine, the oldest living member of The Order, fell ill in August of last year. The class of novices who began their training in the fall was only four in number, and out of those four, not one showed any of the deeper workings of the Holy Spirit. Sister Catherine died this year, on the twentieth of January."

Except for Monica's faint sobs, the room became silent. The sorrow was palpable, the grief in the room, smothering.

"But the purpose of The Order," Patrice said, looking at each woman, then lowering her head, "their special call is to encourage the church during dark times, with prophesies and visions."

Abigail remained silent.

"Someone give Monica a tissue," Sister Kathleen said.

"That's really it?" Patrice asked. "End of story?"

Abigail got up from the table.

"Wait a minute," Sister Kathleen said. "There has to be more."

"And there is," Abigail said. "Sister Catherine left a final prophecy to the community before she died."

"What was it?" Patrice asked.

"That is a question I can not answer at this time, Sisters."

"She's leaving us hanging for another week," Sister Kathleen complained.

"It appears the wait may be much longer. The answer to that question is held by a nun from my community, and until the lines of communication are restored so that she is able to complete her promised visit here to Tranquil Garden, I will wait along with each of you."

Fifteen

Mother Francesca knocked on the door of room 142 before going inside. "Sister Abigail, you asked to see me?"

"I have something to tell you," Abigail said. "I wouldn't have troubled you, but it might be important."

"And what is that?"

"I think I know what happened to Sister Ida's medication. I was with Sister Mary Lawrence when Emily left. I heard Sister Josephine say the taxi driver had taken her up on an offer for a cup of coffee."

"Thank you for letting me know what you heard. I have already dealt with the situation and terminated the nurse responsible. Is there anything else?"

"You fired her? But it was an accident."

"A tragic accident that could bring a tremendous lawsuit against Tranquil Garden. Was there anything else?"

"No, that was all."

Mother Francesca left the room. Turning

toward Clare, Abigail asked, "Did she see the letter?"

Clare pulled a notebook out from under the bedclothes. "I had it hidden." She turned the page and read,

> *"My Dearest Sisters,*
>
> *I grow more concerned by the passing day, and would appreciate immediate word being sent that all is well with each of you. I have not received any correspondence since the letter arrived announcing Sister Alicia's visit, which came to me on the twenty-fourth of January. I pray that Our Lord will soon restore communication between us, as it is now the eleventh of February.*
>
> *His peace be with you,*
>
> *Abigail."*

"Very fine." She handed Clare a worn prayer book and an envelope. "The address is on the inside cover."

"Have your letters surfaced?"

"Sister Janice insists that I threw them away by mistake, but my mind is not so feeble that I believe her." She shook her head. "I save every letter until I return home, then once I am back among my sisters—then and only then—do I throw them away."

"Good morning, Sisters," Nurse Gertie said as she came in pushing her metal cart. "How are we feeling today?"

"I have no complaints," Abigail said.

"You never do." She stopped the cart in the middle of the room. "All this rushing about has made me frazzled. I'm so behind schedule this morning. Why, I don't completely understand. It's not like I've been sitting around. I've put every effort into catching up, but today, Sisters, I don't think anything short of the Lord stopping time will be much help."

"The Lord did that once," Clare said.

Nodding, Abigail said, "It's scriptural."

"Is that right?" Nurse Gertie looked at the women with suspicion. "He really stopped time?"

"If I remember correctly, it's in the Book of Joshua," Abigail said. "The leader of the Israelites wanted more time to properly dispose of the Amorites."

"What is an Amorite?" Nurse Gertie asked.

Clare answered, "They were the nation of people the Israelites were—"

"Were slaughtering," Abigail concluded. "It was definitely a barbaric age."

"This isn't a good subject before taking

blood pressures, Sisters." She removed her equipment from the cart. "Are either of you going to the concert this morning?"

"We both are," Abigail answered. "You should take blood pressures after the concert when everyone is relaxed."

"The stamp is on, Abigail," Clare said as she handed the elderly nun the addressed envelope.

Nurse Gertie wrapped the blood pressure cuff around Clare's arm. "I'll take that letter with me if you want. I can drop it off on Sister Janice's desk when I'm finished."

"Is that where all of our mail goes?" Abigail asked.

"It is," she answered. Nurse Gertie moved the face of her wristwatch in order to see the second hand. "She handles all incoming and outgoing mail and keeps a log of everything."

Abigail sealed the envelope. "I have another letter for Clare to write tomorrow. I think I will wait and keep them together."

"Clare," Nurse Gertie said with excitement. "You have the blood pressure of a teenager." She removed the cuff and wrapped it around Abigail's arm. "Let's see how you're doing this morning."

Abigail smiled. "Even when I was a teenager, I didn't have the blood pressure of one."

She took the reading. "Not so bad today, Abigail. You're doing just fine." Nurse Gertie recorded the information and pushed the metal cart back out into the hallway. "I'll see you at the concert, Sisters."

Clare walked over to the window and looked outside. A brown van with a dented quarter panel rolled slowly past the entrance gate with the driver's side door open. She glanced to the right and saw Tom in his blue coveralls jogging toward the disabled van.

"What do you find more interesting than a bowl of hot oatmeal?"

"It looks like someone's van has broken down outside."

"We shall say a prayer for their vehicle on our way to the dining room."

Clare stepped away from the window as Tom continued to hurry across the grounds. His jog became a fast walk once he cut across the U-shaped driveway.

"Need a hand?" he shouted.

"Hey, Tom. Good to see you."

"What's the matter with her today, George?"

"Beats me." He leaned against the side of the van. "She was driving smooth the whole trip. . . . It's strange."

"What?"

"The minute I see this place I get a bad feeling in my gut and my van gives out on me." He shrugged. "So how is everybody?"

"Doing fine, yourself?"

"Can't complain." George looked into the morning sky. "Great weather today. Last week I was in the Panhandle, outside a little town called Masterson—it's a little more than halfway from Amarillo to Dumas. Anyway, I got caught in an ice storm. It was a mess."

"What were you doing up there?"

"What I'm always doing—playing my music."

Tom said, "We are about as opposite as two people can get. You're never in the same spot for more than a couple of days, and I've been here more years than you've been alive."

"I wouldn't say that, I'm older than you think I am." He ran his hand along his jet-black hair, then tugged at his ponytail. "Forty-three next month."

"That does cut it close. I've been here almost thirty-five years."

"Same place for thirty-five years—man, I could never have done that."

"What are you playing today?"

"Don't know yet."

Tom laughed. "The Sisters would probably like rock and roll if *you* were playing it."

"I don't play rock. Don't like it, don't play it." George took a guitar pick from his jeans pocket. "Don't let the long hair fool you. It's not about rock music, it's about keeping myself from going bald."

"You lost me, George. How can growing

your hair long change whether or not you go bald?"

George leaned his head back and looked into the sky. "All of the men in my family were nearly bald by the time they hit thirty years of age. I decided when I turned twenty-one that since I wasn't going to have it for long, I wasn't going to cut it again. My brother did the same thing, but he got tired of it after a few years. Yep, he got a haircut, and within six months the whole top of his head was shiny smooth."

"Yeah?"

"True story. I'm the only male member of my family—second and third cousins included—who still has hair on the top of his head." George ran his hand along the side of his bearded face. "Now the beard, the beard is another story."

Tom kicked at a bug. "You grew it to keep your eyelashes from falling out."

"Naw, I grew it because I'm ugly." George smiled. "Are you up to helping me push her down the driveway?"

The men pushed the van slowly up the long driveway; then George unloaded his black guitar case and headed for the activity room. About fifty folding chairs had been set up facing a lone stool. He would not need a music stand; everything he played came from either his memory or his heart. As he took the instrument into his hands, his eyes would close, and the memory of the song would come alive in his fingertips.

At the appointed time, when the room was filled, George began to play. He moved his fingers effortlessly among the strings. Today he used his thumb and two middle fingers in a fingerpick style of guitar playing. The classical masters would not approve, but that did not matter to George. What mattered to him was that the women sitting in front of him were all being soothed by the gentle melodies flowing from his guitar.

For an hour he played as the nuns listened, then he looked around the room. "Before I close things up, I was told Mother Francesca would like to make an announcement."

She came to the front of the room. "As you know, Sisters, Tranquil Garden has been a gift to the religious world, providing a peaceful environment for you to spend the remaining years of your vocations. And it will continue to be regardless of the labors of any single person."

The Sisters began to whisper.

Mother Francesca signaled for silence. "There have been some rumors circulating that I will be stepping down from my duties as Superior General of the Sisters of Mercy. They are true."

"No, Mother," a nun said.

Another Sister stood up. "You must stay."

"Please, Sisters!" Mother Francesca said.

"I feel the closeness that you feel and will grieve our separation when I accept my new assignment at our foundation in Phoenix on the first of April. We must think of our community here at Tranquil Garden. It is time for the young to assume their leadership roles."

The Sisters silently accepted the news. Mother Francesca left the room flanked by Sisters of Mercy and other staff members who had tear-filled eyes. The nurses and aides began helping the residents back to their rooms. Abigail stood for a moment with Sister Kathleen and Monica, then made her way over to George. "Good morning, young man."

"Good morning, Sister."

"You play your guitar like an angel."

"Thank you," he said. "Sometimes I'm playing and I get lost inside the music." He shrugged. "I guess that doesn't make any sense."

"Indeed it does. Your music is your prayer."

George smiled. "I like that. Thank you, Sister."

Abigail reached into her pocket. "Could I ask a favor of you?"

"Sure."

She offered the letter. "Could you mail this for me?"

Taking the envelope, George looked at the address. "I've been to Massachusetts. It sure gets cold up there." He put the letter into his back pocket. "I'd be happy to mail it for you, Sister."

"Thank you, young man."

Abigail wore a confident smile as she left the room. George put his guitar into its case with tenderness and headed into the hallway.

His boots announced every step with echoing clumps against the white tile floor. The staff offices came into view. He knocked on Mother Francesca's door.

"Come on in and sit down, George," she said. "I thought your check was already prepared, but I was mistaken. It will only take a moment."

"I'm in no hurry. Tom said I could borrow some tools. My van gave out on me before the concert."

"You are welcome to anything we have. Tom can show you where everything is kept."

"I appreciate the help."

Mother Francesca took a binder from the bookcase over to her desk. "And we appreciate you."

"Is there a mailbox around here?"

"Four miles up the highway there is a gas station. They have a mailbox right outside, but I don't believe they pick up more than twice a week. We have daily service here at Tranquil Garden. If the matter is important, you can give the letter to me, and I'll be happy to mail it for you."

George reached into his back pocket. "That's all right, she asked me to mail it for her."

Mother Francesca looked up from the binder. "She?"

George looked at the envelope again. "I think it says *Abigail.*"

"May I see that, please?"

"Here."

She took the envelope into her hands. "I must apologize. We've had our hands full with Sister Abigail lately. We have a strict protocol for handling correspondence, and she has become rather difficult about it."

George held out his hand for the envelope. "It's no trouble. I have to stop for gas anyway."

"I'm afraid I must insist. Abigail is under our care and authority and she must abide by our way of doing things." She tore out a check. "Here you are. We'll see you next month."

George picked up his guitar case and left the office. Mother Francesca tapped the envelope against her desk for several minutes before getting up and walking to room 142.

"Sister Abigail, what am I to do with you?" She displayed the blur of an envelope to her. "Why did you give George this letter to mail?"

Abigail's hands began to tremble. "Because Sister Janice has not been mailing my letters, and she has not been giving me my arriving letters."

Mother Francesca walked over and studied Abigail closely. "How long has it been since you received a letter from your convent?"

"The twenty-fourth of January, and they are of the custom of writing me daily."

"I will get to the bottom of this the minute Sister Janice returns, but until then, I want the disobedience to stop." Abigail responded with nod. "Please do not test my patience any further."

Sixteen

Clare pushed open the wooden door leading to the Critical Care Unit and saw the same brunette nurse she had seen there before. Looking up from her post at the nurses' station, the woman eyed the elderly nun with curiosity. "It's four o'clock in the morning, sweetie. You should be in bed." She waited for Clare to say something. "Did you come to sit with someone?"

"I am to go into that room."

"Sister Ida is in there." The nurse motioned with a pencil. "You go right on in."

Clare covered the distance slowly and entered the room. The open door cast enough light for her to see a place to sit near the bed. She let go of the door and found her way to a straight-backed chair. With the exception of the lights coming from a heart monitor and a dim light just above the bed, the room was dark.

"Who's there?" Sister Ida asked.

"My name is Clare."

"My death is approaching."

"Yes," Clare said gently.

"I have wondered about this day since my thirtieth birthday, when I was given the understanding that I would one day experience death. That was a difficult day. I would have preferred remaining invincible at least another year. I prayed that day with more fervor than I have ever prayed. I asked to be able to walk through death without fear, that when my Lord came to me at the conclusion of my life, I would greet Him only with joy."

"And are you afraid?" Clare asked gently.

"I surely and truly am not."

"And are you filled with joy?"

"It is as though I am bursting with it."

"Then I would say that prayer has been answered."

Sister Ida smiled weakly. "My pain grows less and less, and although I can hear the sounds of my body fighting for breath, it seems easier and easier to breathe. The time is near."

"And He is near."

"Please loosen me from all of this machinery. Take me to Him that my joy may be complete."

"He has chosen to come to you, Ida."

As she spoke, a sound of music, at first faint, grew louder. The form of a man approached the bedside. Ida's radiant face looked upon her gentle Lord as He placed His hands beneath her, lifting her from the bed. Love-filled tears glistened His cheeks and His beard as He turned slowly and carried Ida further into the brightness that surrounded them.

Clare sat quietly in the darkened room until the door to the hallway opened, sending a bright flash of light across the room. Someone switched on the overhead light. She shielded her eyes with the back of her hand and blinked furiously in an attempt to help her eyes adjust.

"Let's get you back to your room," the brunette nurse said.

The woman led Clare to a wheelchair waiting in the hallway.

"Take your time getting in."

Clare took hold of an armrest and maneuvered her way into the chair. "What is your name?"

"Brenda Peterson. Yours?"

"Clare."

"Where are we going?" Brenda asked.

"My room number is 142."

"That is quite a walk from Critical Care." She turned into the east/west hallway. "Smell that sausage? One of my favorite things is cooking. Actually, being a cook was my second career choice, but nursing school was a safer place for me. I was never very adept with a knife. I can sauté and fry with the best of them, but chopping and slicing aren't good ideas for me." The nurse nodded to a coworker walking by. "It's funny how things work out. I actually got to do both things I loved doing the most. I had seven children, all picky eaters—and believe me, Sister, cooking for them is an experience."

"I'm sure it is."

"Then when my youngest child started high school I dusted off my old nursing degree, got re-certified, and came to work here. What was your second career choice?"

Clare folded her hands in her lap. "I didn't have one."

"You never wanted to be anything else?"

"Even as a child, all I wanted was to live apart from the world, but serve the Lord in the world, and the best way for Him to grant that in my life was to call me into a religious community."

"I think that is so wonderful. I've always admired nuns."

"You did the same in your life," Clare said quickly. "We just had different living arrangements. Your family is your community, your house is your convent, and your service is your nursing. We are not so different."

"I've always pictured convents as quiet, peaceful, and clean," she said. "My house was always full of arguing children, and my sinks always seemed to be piled with dishes that needed to be washed."

"Once our community invited the local bishop to celebrate a dedication Mass after they remodeled our chapel. At the last minute we were told he would arrive early to bless the rooms of the convent with holy water. We were already overrun with visitors, and tensions were high that morning. We all rushed about dusting and polishing, and we sounded very much like a house full of arguing children. Our minds were so preoccupied with our rushing and our squabbling that we didn't realize until the bishop's car was pulling into the driveway that our breakfast dishes had not been washed and put away."

"What did you do?"

"We stacked them up and hid them on closet shelves."

"I hope the bishop didn't bless the closets."

She laughed hard. "I will never forget the look on our Superior General's face. She was absolutely mortified."

"I've hidden dishes in the oven before, but I never thought of hiding them in closets. I'll remember that one." She stopped outside the door of room 142. "I'll let you out here so we won't disturb your roommate. Thank you for the story, Sister."

Clare got out of the wheelchair and waited by the door until Brenda was on her way back to the Critical Care Unit. She pushed the door open. The bright light from the hall pierced the room. She stepped inside and closed the door behind her. As she walked toward her bed, Clare noticed that Abigail was not snoring.

"Did I wake you?" she asked.

"I forgot the number," Abigail said with a sigh. She sat up and felt for the lamp on the night table. "I woke up and tried to recall the phone number, but it's completely gone from my memory. All day long I could recite it perfectly. I could practically recite it backwards."

"Think of something else," Clare suggested.

Abigail closed her eyes. "There—I am thinking of something else." A moment passed. "How long shall I do this?"

"I don't know."

Abigail opened her eyes. "You don't know?"

"You think of something else until the number comes back to you."

"And if it doesn't, child?"

"Then we will spend more patient hours learning the number again."

"St. Michael's monastery in Philadelphia," Abigail said. "You led the women's retreat on Teresa of Avila's *Interior Castle.*"

"I've never been to Philadelphia."

Abigail raised her eyebrows as she accepted the answer. "I see you were off on one of your pre-dawn excursions. The peace of Jesus flows from you. It would be safe to assume that we are one fewer in number here at Tranquil Garden."

"We are," Clare said. She took off her robe. "Sister Ida died."

Abigail laid down. "How hard it is not to be envious. How I long for my final day."

"To desire that day alone is to be blinded to this day," Clare said as she got into bed. "The Lord has a purpose for your remaining days, Abigail; otherwise He would not have given them to you."

Seventeen

Sister Janice walked into room 142 with her hands behind her back. "I have a surprise for you, Sister Abigail." She brought her hands back around. "Letters! Nearly a dozen of them. There must have been a backlog at the post office."

"They are only blurs to me, Sister. May I hold them?"

She gave the old woman the letters. "It's good to see you smile again."

Abigail wept as she clutched the envelopes. She cleared her throat. "And I will savor every word in each precious one."

"Shall I read them to you?"

Abigail shook her head. "I am worn out from the weeks of worry. Clare will read them to me later."

Sister Janice left. The room became silent except for the tearing sounds of envelopes opening. "Clare? Are you still in there?"

The bathroom door opened. "I lost another hair pin while I was securing my headpiece."

"I am surprised that water can still travel down that drain at all with the number of pins you have lost since your arrival. You know where I keep them—help yourself, child."

Clare made her way to the bureau and retrieved a pin. "What are those?"

"They are glorious letters from my community. Will you please read one to me when you are finished in there?"

"If this pin stays in place, I am finished." She came over to the sitting area. "Which one do you want me to read first?"

Abigail handed her a piece of light blue stationery. "This one."

"Dearest Abigail,

How lucky you are to be in such a warm climate. The days are dismally cold as is to be expected in winter. We miss your cheerful presence among us and look forward to your return in March.

God bless you,

Sister Mary Margaret."

"That is odd."
Clare looked up. "What?"
"We have no Sister Mary Margaret in our community." Abigail opened another envelope. "Something is not right. Try this one."

"To our dear Abigail,

As we continue in this Lenten season we look forward to the celebration of our risen Lord, and to your return to us. Please continue to pray for us, and know that you are in our prayers.

Sincerely in Christ,

The Sisters of the Divine Name."

"Something is wrong. Those are not the letters from my community. There is no intimacy in them. They were written by someone who does not know me. Sister Martha and I were discussing our struggles with pride, and how the Lord in His immense patience was still hopeful of refining a bit more of the golden fruit of humility in both of us at our ripe old ages. Another Sister was struggling over whether or not to take her permanent vows in May. They wrote to me about intimate things, not things like this."

"These don't have your community's letterhead," said Clare as she examined both sides of the stationery. "And this paper—it's not the same either."

Abigail adjusted her glasses. "The postmark. Where are the postmarks from?"

Clare went through the envelopes. "Houston, Houston, all of them are Houston except this one. It is more local, it says Freeport."

"Open that one, child."

"Dear Abigail,

I haven't found a job yet, but I thought I would write anyway. I've applied at a few places, and I don't think it will be long before I have an offer. I'll never forget that afternoon at the fountain.

Thanks again, and take care,

Dorothy."

"It seems I can receive mail. Dorothy's letter proves that. But do they have to manufacture letters from my community? That makes no sense, unless . . ." She put her hand on her forehead. "Have I been abandoned?"

"No, Abigail, they would never abandon you."

"I am completely cut off from them, and I don't know why." She closed her eyes and remained silent for several minutes. "I can't endure this agony. I will wait no longer. I must attempt another call."

"I will go with you."

"Put those letters into the drawer of the night table where the others were in case someone comes hunting through my things again," Abigail directed. She waited for Clare to help her from the chair. "Let us be on our way."

Clare looked to her right as they entered the hallway. "Someone left a wheelchair."

"A godsend for this weary body, but I must pass up the opportunity. An offered wheelchair carries no penalty, a chosen one does. I can not risk being moved from this wing."

"We will be at the dining room soon."

"I am interested in discovering why Sister Janice wrote all those letters."

"You think she wrote them?"

"I'm certain she did. And she mailed them earlier in the week during her trip to Houston. There have been some strange happenings since I received the letter announcing Sister Alicia's arrival with the words of Sister Catherine's final prophecy. It is as if something is interfering with every attempt at communication, and I would like to know what that something is."

"It might be best not to know."

"If it involves the powers of darkness— and I am beginning to believe it does—you are right. May this one finally be a successful mission."

Clare led Abigail to the phone and picked up the handset. She secured the phone within Abigail's grasp, then pushed the buttons. "Nine—zero—there, is it ringing?"

"Sister Abigail!" Sister Judith called from the back entrance. "You know you aren't supposed to be using that phone. Go out to the visiting area and make your call from Sister Janice's desk."

"I will not," she said strongly.

"But you must. Sister Janice has to keep a record so the calls can be correctly billed. You know the procedure."

"I am making a collect call. There is no need of record keeping."

Sister Judith thought through Abigail's response. "All right—I guess you can go ahead."

"Clare, if you would place the call to the operator again?"

"Of course." She pushed the buttons. "There you go."

"Yes, operator, I would like to place a collect call."

Sister Judith bent over toward Clare and whispered, "I'm not sure how Mother Francesca will feel about this. Please encourage Abigail to make any other calls through Sister Janice."

"I will do that." Clare watched as Sister Judith left the dining room. "Did you get through?"

"It's ringing now," Abigail said. "Yes, I am still here, operator. Could you give it a few more rings, please? Thank you."

"What's wrong?"

"There is no answer." Abigail shook her head. "What time is it?"

Clare looked around the room until she spotted a clock mounted over the entrance to the kitchen. "It is one-thirty."

"What time would it be in Massachusetts?"

"Two-thirty."

"That explains why—What? Yes, operator, I will try again later. Thank you." She gave the handset back to Clare. "A strict silence is kept in the community from noon until three o'clock. I will have to make another call later."

"Sister Judith told me to instruct you to make any other calls through Sister Janice."

"Then consider me so instructed. Let us start on our way back to our room before we are discovered again."

Clare took hold of Abigail's arm. As they reached the entrance to the dining room, Abigail asked, "Who is that?"

"It's Graciella."

"Good afternoon, child."

"May the peace of the Lord cover you this day, Abigail."

"And you, Graciella."

"Are you on your way to the sanctuary for prayer, dear one?"

"I will join you after I return."

"There is no need for you to wear yourself out walking back and forth," Abigail said. "You go on, and I will see you later."

"It's no trouble."

"It is, and I will not ask it of you. I enjoy the company, but this old body is still capable of making the journey alone." She let go of Clare's arm. "It is a relief to see you and Graciella meeting for prayer at a more reasonable hour instead of running off when it is time for a meal. Go on, child."

Clare walked across the hallway and opened the door to the sanctuary. Taking a seat next to Graciella, she began to quiet herself. The moments passed slowly, gently. The intimate communication between Clare and her Lord went unnoticed by Graciella, just as Graciella's went unnoticed by Clare. There would be no distractions made or disturbances caused. Each enjoyed the silent moments of prayer.

When the time arrived for the women to leave, Graciella turned toward Clare. "I believe you received a word from the Lord."

"I did."

"I, too, received a word. I'm sure they are one and the same. Listen, dear one, and tell me if I received them correctly: 'The innocent will perish in the fires set by trusted hands. But fear not, for out of these ashes will arise new life and greater glory for My Name.'"

"You received it correctly."

"Are these the words of the prophecy Abigail has been waiting to receive?"

"Yes," Clare agreed. "And there is more."

"A vision," Graciella said softly. "Which will be given to Abigail at the hour appointed by the Lord." She stood up. "Come, dear one. Let us deliver the words of the prophecy."

Eighteen

When Sister Kathleen came into the work-room, she eyed an empty seat. "Where's Abigail?"

"I don't know," Clare said. "She canceled our weekly reading after only two verses, and excused herself once Sister Janice left the room."

"How long has she been gone?" Sister Kathleen asked.

"About forty-five minutes."

Monica took her seat at the table. "It's not like Abigail to be late. She's hardly ever been late for making rosaries. What if something happened to her?"

"Maybe we should go and check the stair-wells," Patrice suggested.

Sister Kathleen pointed her finger at her. "Sister Patrice, don't even think such a thing."

"Well," said Patrice, "something is going on."

"Abigail never misses one of our meetings," Monica said. "I think we should look for her."

"I don't think the Lord would want anyone ending up in Critical Care over the stress of all this," said Sister Kathleen. "Let's take a minute of silence, Sisters, and pray for a little direction."

The room became silent as they bowed their heads. The moments passed until one by one, each nun looked up.

"Graciella, check the sanctuary," Sister Kathleen said. "Clare: the courtyard, Monica: the visiting area. Patrice: you and I will check the—just come with me."

Monica felt her legs begin to tremble. "You're going to check the stairwells!"

"Never mind about that, you go on to the visiting room. Everyone meet back here after you've checked your area."

"What if we don't find her?" Monica asked.

"Then we will notify Mother Francesca," Sister Kathleen said. "And they will find her."

Clare followed the rest of the nuns out of the room and headed for the courtyard. Once outside, she checked Abigail's usual spot on the wooden bench. It was empty. She moved along swiftly, stopping at the iron fence that enclosed one side of the courtyard.

The heels of her black tennis shoes raised into the air as she peered over the fence. The sight of the old woman walking slowly toward the building brought Clare both relief and concern. Relief that she was all right, and concern that Mother Francesca or Sister Janice might discover Abigail before she returned to the courtyard. Clare lifted the gate latch and hurried to meet her.

"Beautiful day for a walk, Abigail."

"I would enjoy staying out here for the rest of the afternoon, but we have rosaries to make."

"I see that I am not the only one taking excursions around here. I hope it was a pleasant one."

"I will tell you where I have been, if you are asking?"

"I would never pry into your private affairs."

Abigail reached for Clare's arm. "Am I late for our meeting?"

"You are. We are all scouring the building for you."

"We? Are Mother Francesca and Sister Janice looking for me?"

"No—at least, they weren't when I left."

"Good, they can both do without the worry of it. It was a short excursion, one I was quite capable of completing alone—as you are currently witnessing." She looked up toward the building. "What does Tranquil Garden look like?"

"It looks very big with its white walls and Spanish architecture. Near each window you can see colored trails where water running off the ledge has stained the wall."

"Are the roof tiles really as red as my blurs make them seem?"

"More of a faded red."

"The Lord humbles us in interesting ways."

Clare nodded. "Yes, He does."

"On the afternoon when you and Graciella arrived from the sanctuary with the words of the final prophecy, I was gloriously astounded. My spirit leapt with joy. Then, you both informed me of the vision that was to come, the vision I was to receive. I have never had a vision in the whole of my life. I have not even been blessed with any spiritual dreams, or the imagination to contemplate such things."

"You doubted."

"*Doubted* is not a strong enough word in this case."

Clare looked closely at Abigail as she opened the courtyard gate. "You have received the promised vision."

"I have. While I was looking out over the gulf, listening to the roar of the moving water, the Lord saw fit to grant this lowly creature the vision He assured you He would send to me."

"Monica! Monica!" Sister Kathleen called from the courtyard entrance. "Sister Abigail is right here, and she seems just fine."

Monica looked out the glass door. "I'm going to tell the others."

"Tell them to be seated and to be ready for listening," Abigail said in a loud voice. "I have much to tell them today."

Returning to the workroom, the Sisters assembled around the table. Monica distributed the supplies hurriedly, her eyes watching Abigail's every move. There was something different about the old woman this afternoon; a deep calm surrounded her.

"I will begin today, Sisters, with the words of the final prophecy that we have been awaiting together."

"It's about time you heard from your community," Sister Kathleen said.

Monica smiled. "I knew the Lord would answer our prayers."

"The streams of communication are still dried up, Sisters, and your prayers are even more urgently needed—you will discover this as the story progresses."

"How did you get the words of the prophecy?" Monica asked.

"The Lord is a masterful engineer. The streams of communication to my community were completely blocked and remain so to this present time. Yet the Lord located two vessels in another channel that were able to deliver the cargo."

Patrice grimaced. "Vessels, channels, cargo. What are you talking about?"

"She's speaking figuratively," Sister Kathleen said sharply. "Anyone with any sense knows that." She looked at Abigail. "Those vessels were some of us."

"*Two* of us," Patrice argued. "She said two vessels."

"Graciella was one," Sister Kathleen said quickly. "And—and it must have been Monica too."

"I would have been honored, but it wasn't."

Sister Kathleen looked around. "Then it was Clare."

"It doesn't matter," Patrice said in a loud voice. "Let her go ahead with the story."

Abigail hunted through her plastic bag until she gripped a black bead. "These are the words of the Lord: 'The innocent will perish in the fires set by trusted hands. But fear not, for out of these ashes will arise new life and greater glory for My Name.'"

Monica twisted a piece of wire around the end of her pliers and formed a loop. "The innocent will perish? Who will perish, Abigail?"

"That I do not know, but there is more."

Sister Kathleen looked over her glasses. "Tell us."

"The messengers of this prophecy also announced that our Lord would bestow upon me a vision concerning The Order."

"That's why the Lord's radiance is upon you," Monica said. "You've had a vision!"

"I was called by our Lord to venture outside and journey to that great body of water referred to as the Gulf of Mexico. I stood and looked, and as I looked I noticed that I could see the water clearly. I watched waves form and flow inland, then recede back into the beautiful water."

"Oh, Abigail," Monica sighed. "How delightful for you."

"With this clear picture in front of me, I received the realization that I was indeed having a vision. I looked down to the sand, and there I saw an old brown withered leaf exactly as it was described in the vision received by those of The Order, which they had on their third day of prayer and fasting following the removal of Sister Theresa."

"Did you see the young leaves?" Patrice asked. "They also saw young leaves."

Sister Kathleen sent a sharp look in Patrice's direction. "Let her finish."

"There before me was the old withered leaf," Abigail continued. "I was gripped by how clearly I was seeing the texture of this leaf. Every vein and curved edge was visible to me. I could see nothing else, only the sand and the leaf. Then, I saw two hands, gentle and young. They picked up and held the leaf. After a few moments, I saw the old leaf break apart as if crushed by some heavy object, although it remained in the palms of these delicate and soft-looking hands."

"Precious Lord," Monica moaned.

"The hands left my sight, taking with them the pieces of the old, withered leaf. It was then I saw that beneath the leaf, was another."

"The young green leaf," Patrice said.

Sister Kathleen turned her head quickly. "Let her finish."

"On the contrary, this leaf was even older and more withered than the one that had been above it. Slowly, the leaf that remained began to transform before my eyes into a lush green leaf more vibrant than any still attached to the branch of a tree. It was a sight that will not easily be forgotten." Abigail coughed, then cleared her throat. "I continued to watch as young, tender green leaves appeared one at a time around the leaf that had been old and withered. One by one they appeared until there were eleven encircling the larger one."

"What does it mean?" Monica asked.

"Of only one thing am I certain," Abigail said slowly. "I am convinced The Order exists still, and will be fully restored."

"I don't see it," Sister Kathleen said flatly. "With Sister Catherine dead there is no Order."

"One still remains," Graciella announced.

All heads turned toward Graciella and waited for further words. When none came, Monica looked over to Abigail and said, "Novice

Rachel. Could the bottom leaf be Novice Rachel?"

Abigail smiled. "I believe it is."

"But where is she?" Sister Kathleen said. "Anything could have happened to her. She could be living in Tampa, Florida, baby-sitting her grandchildren."

"I think she joined another religious community," Monica said.

"I agree," Abigail said. "Which is precisely why I must double my efforts to restore communications with my community. My sisters must be informed so that Rachel can be located and restored to The Order."

"What can we do to help?" Sister Kathleen asked.

"Besides your prayers, I truly do not know. I believe the powers of darkness have a hand in this communication breakdown."

"Then why don't we try to find Rachel ourselves?" Monica asked. "What was her hometown?"

"If I can trust this old memory of mine, I believe it was Tulsa, Oklahoma."

Sister Kathleen pointed her pliers for emphasis. "You can't tell me that out of all of these nuns here at Tranquil Garden there isn't one who doesn't have some kind of connection with Tulsa, Oklahoma. There are records that could be checked, or a relative could be found. We might even have some Sisters from a community with a convent there."

"Our efforts would best be spent in prayer," said Abigail. "We must trust the Lord to reveal Rachel at the hour He appoints. We should not put ourselves on this path where the Lord has not called us to walk. Remember, Sisters, there will be dangers ahead. Let us progress only at the direction of the Lord."

"What do you mean, *dangers?*" Sister Kathleen asked.

"'The innocent will perish,'" Monica said fearfully. "The words of the final prophecy."

Sister Kathleen looked slowly around the table. "Sisters, it looks like this story is taking on a life of its own."

Nineteen

Good morning," said Nurse Gertie cheerfully. "How are we feeling today?"

"We are hungry," Abigail answered. "I am eager for my warm bowl of oatmeal."

Nurse Gertie rolled her cart into the room. "The hallway outside the dining room was full of the smell of bacon frying. I think I'd rather have some of that."

Abigail shook her head. "I prefer my oatmeal."

"She has a bowl every morning," Clare said. "Faithfully."

Nurse Gertie lifted the stethoscope from around her neck. "Who wants to have their blood pressure taken first?"

Abigail motioned with her hand. "You may start with me. I am feeling very good this morning, and may even rival Clare's reading today."

She wrapped the fabric cuff around Abigail's thin arm and took the reading. "This is an improvement." She removed the cuff and wrote the numbers on a clipboard that hung from a small hook on the side of the cart. "A tremendous improvement." She moved over to Clare and wrapped the cuff around her arm. "Let's see how you're doing." She took the reading. "Steady as always. I saw on the chart that you were brought a pain reliever last night. That's four Sundays in a row. Is everything all right?"

"It was nothing. I had a headache."

"She has one every Sunday night."

Nurse Gertie put her hand on her ample hip. "Is that true?"

"Yes," Clare answered.

"We better have someone take a look at you."

"There's no need."

Nurse Gertie wrote on the clipboard. "Yes, there is. We need to find out what is causing those headaches."

"I am allergic to cheese," Clare said simply.

"And all that is available for dinner on Sundays are those delicious casseroles with cheese sauces," Abigail explained.

The nurse took the clipboard from the cart again. "They can do something about that in the kitchen. I'm sure they can make something else for you."

"There's no need for special arrangements," Clare said. "I enjoy the food. And one dose of aspirin each week is not a concern to me."

Abigail got up from her chair. "It is probably doing her some good."

Nurse Gertie thumbed through the pages on her clipboard. "You aren't on any other medications." She scratched through what she had written. "All right, but if it becomes a problem, you just let me know." She wheeled the cart toward the hallway, then stopped in the doorway. "Oh, Sister Clare, did you locate Sister Gloria?"

"I was told she had been moved. Again."

"Getting a second-floor resident settled sometimes takes a bit of doing. Try room 218. I hear she has the room all to herself."

"Thank you. I will plan to see her this afternoon."

"A visit will definitely do her a lot of good."

"Is she ill?" Abigail asked with concern.

"She's having some emotional problems. It's not all that unusual. The adjustment into a nursing home is a tough one, and the arthritis has isolated her from the others. I'll bet your visit this afternoon is just the medicine she needs. Enjoy your breakfast, Sisters."

Clare placed her hand on Abigail's shoulder as the two left the room. "I'll meet you for breakfast later."

"Not that I am prying into your personal affairs, but would it be reasonable to assume that you are on your way to see Gloria?"

"I won't be long."

"I'll have them save you a bowl of oatmeal."

"Thank you, but I'm really not one for oatmeal."

"The oatmeal I can take or leave," Abigail said as a smile stretched across her face. "It's the warmed maple syrup I can't do without."

Clare turned to go the other way. She walked quietly up the stairwell at the end of the hall. The upper floor was empty except for a Sister of Mercy who was sitting in a chair outside the room at the furthest end of the hall. As she approached the far end of the hall, Clare noticed that none of the doors to the rooms were open, as they usually were on the first floor. No one could be seen walking the hall. She heard no sound of conversation or laughter coming from any of the rooms. There seemed to be no life at all.

Sister Angelica looked up from the book she was reading. She was a young nun, not past twenty-five, with bright red hair and a generous splash of freckles on her cheeks. "Where are you going?"

Clare raised her hand and pointed toward the door. "Into that room."

"I'm afraid I can't let you do that, Sister Clare," she said gently. "You are Sister Clare?"

"I am."

Sister Angelica closed the book and stood up. She was a tall woman and towered over Clare. "Sister Gloria is on restriction today. She can't have any visitors. You can try again tomorrow."

Clare turned around without argument.

She made her way back downstairs to the dining room. "Good morning, Robert," she said.

Robert smiled. "You're running late this morning, Sister. We're out of bacon, but I have some link sausage."

"With eggs, please."

Robert passed the plate under the glass. "There you go."

She poured a cup of coffee and took her tray to table nine.

"Who is that?" Abigail asked.

"It's Clare," Monica said. "We're glad to see you."

Abigail moved her fork and knife closer to her bowl of oatmeal. "How did your visiting expedition go?"

Her expression saddened. "They are keeping me from seeing her."

Sister Kathleen leaned over toward Patrice. "What are they talking about?"

"Be quiet, and we'll all be able to hear."

Clare began cutting her link sausage into pieces. "I was politely told that Gloria can't have any visitors."

"No visitors?" Monica gasped. "Why?"

"She's been put on restriction."

Sister Kathleen moved her chair closer to Abigail. "What are you two talking about?"

"Clare was finally able to locate one of her community members. She was hoping to be able to see her this morning."

Patrice asked, "Why didn't you see her?"

"She's been put on restriction," Clare repeated. "I was told she couldn't have any visitors."

"Can they do that?" Patrice asked.

Abigail gathered the syrup that clung to the bottom of her bowl. "It seems they can do whatever they wish. I think I will make a trip up to room 218."

Monica set down a nearly empty glass of milk. "But what if you walk all that way only to get turned around at the door?"

"The exercise will do me good," said Abigail as she took the cloth napkin that was draped across her lap and wiped her mouth. "And I think it's important that we learn why Sister Gloria is on this restriction, and how long they intend for this isolation to continue."

"I will go with you," Monica offered.

Abigail guided her chair back and stood up. "I will go alone, but do, all of you, accompany me with your prayers."

The old woman made her way out of the dining room and over to the elevator located behind Sister Janice's desk. She felt along the wall for the button to summon her ride to the second floor.

A sharp ding rang out, and the elevator door opened.

"Watch your step," said a woman, who smelled strongly of perfume. She led Abigail into the wide elevator and pushed another button. The compartment rose smoothly. "Here you are, Sister. Take your time. I'll hold the door for as long as you need."

"Aren't you coming out?"

"No, I was only along for the ride."

"I thank you for the help. Do you know where I can find room 218?"

"To the right; you're not far."

The metal door closed and the old woman began walking down the hallway. She spotted a large blur near one of the rooms. "Good morning," she called out.

"Good morning," Sister Angelica said warmly. Her blue eyes sparkled. "Can I help you?"

"I hope so. I'm looking for room 218. Do you know where it is?"

"It's right here."

"Good, then my trip is over."

The young nun snapped her book closed and stood up. "Let me get the door for you." She opened the door and led Abigail inside. "Sister Gloria, I brought a visitor with me."

The bedridden nun lifted her head briefly from the two thick pillows that supported it. "Can you stay for a little while, Sister?"

Abigail touched along the edge of the bed until she felt Gloria's cold hand. She grasped it firmly. "I can stay."

Sister Angelica sat in a chair by the far

wall. Minutes passed silently. The young nun read from the pages of her book while Abigail continued to hold Gloria's hand.

A beeping sound suddenly filled the room.

"What is that?" Gloria asked with alarm.

Sister Angelica came to the side of the bed and tenderly stroked Gloria's head. "It's only my beeper. I have to go to the nurses' station and answer the page." She looked at Abigail. "Will you stay with her until I get back?"

"I will."

The door closed behind Sister Angelica with a clank. Gloria gripped Abigail's hand more firmly. "Please, Sister, I must get a message to someone on the first floor. I haven't much time—please listen carefully. I must get a message to Clare. She is from the Sisters of the Sacred Heart community. Her room number is 142."

"Yes, yes child, she is my roommate."

"Oh—Praise be to Jesus!" She ran her tongue across her dry lips. "I must be quick, before Sister Angelica returns. Warn Clare—tell her—they intend to kill each of us who arrived from the Sisters of the Sacred Heart community. Florence was first, I will be next, and then Clare."

Abigail's voice shook with emotion. "Why? Do you know why?"

Gloria's head shook from side to side. "I pray and pray, but it has not been given to me to understand. I only know that evil governs one within these walls. Please—you must warn her."

"At once." She stroked Gloria's hand. "Calm yourself. With the Lord's help I will find a way to get Clare safely away from this place—but no more words now, child. Someone is coming."

Sister Angelica walked into the room. "I think you should sit down, Sister Abigail. I have some news to pass along that you may find disturbing: Sister Janice from the main desk just called up here looking for you." Abigail lowered herself back into the chair. "We just received word from the hospital. Sister Emily died early this morning."

"We will miss her." Abigail closed her eyes for a moment. "Will there be a memorial service?"

"Yes, but it isn't scheduled." Sister Angelica studied Abigail closely. "Are you all right?"

"This loss tears at my heart. But the Lord strengthens all who rely on Him." She raised herself from the chair. "May I visit Sister Gloria tomorrow?"

"If you'd like. Earlier is better for her. The medications she's on are very strong, and she tends to ramble on about things that don't make sense."

Abigail gave Gloria's hand a squeeze before letting go. "I can assure you, she did no rambling this morning. None at all."

Twenty

Clare probed the sink drain with her fingers after dropping a hair pin. The search was useless. Another one had fallen beyond her grasp. She reached into a ceramic bowl, put next to the soap dish by Abigail to save Clare a journey back to the dresser, and selected a second hair pin.

A sudden noise caught her attention. She opened the bathroom door a crack and listened. She heard it again and went out into the hallway to investigate. "Abigail, are you all right?" she said, upon seeing her roommate.

"My visit to the second floor was more of a journey than I realized." She took hold of Clare's arm. "Have you heard about Emily?"

"Sister Janice just told me."

"A senseless tragedy," Abigail said. "Ironically, she had been concerned about *me* before her departure. I regret she wasted the energy seeing how adept I am at worrying about my own situation." An expression of frustration gripped her face as she sat in her chair. "Will I ever get beyond the self-centeredness that rules not only my actions, but my thoughts?"

"No."

Abigail laughed heartily. "Indeed, I suppose I am a hopeless case."

"Not hopeless, human." Clare went over to the dresser and retrieved another hairpin. "Did you see Gloria?"

"I was led into her room by Sister Angelica herself."

"I don't understand. I was clearly turned away."

"Something strange is going on here," Abigail said. "Is Gloria known to excite easily?"

"Actually, she is one of the most balanced people I know."

"She is concerned for you," said Abigail.

Clare remained silent.

"I would advise that you stay away from Gloria's room for the time being. It was Sister Angelica who turned you away, correct?"

"Yes, she specifically said Gloria was on restriction and could not have any visitors."

Abigail rubbed her hands together as if they were cold. "I have a growing discomfort about all of this, but there is nothing more I can do."

"When Sister Janice stopped by to bring the news about Sister Emily, she said she was unable to reach your convent again today. She said she'd try a little earlier tomorrow."

"As much as I appreciate her efforts to

save me the lengthy walk, I am wondering about these phone calls made on my behalf." She pushed herself up. "Would you join me? I am feeling a bit unsteady today."

Clare took hold of her arm. "Are you sure you don't want to take a longer rest?"

"It seems I have walked further in the last week than all of the distance I have covered in the last year, and, oddly enough, I think I feel the better for it."

"Frequent walks are good for the heart," Clare said as they started down the hallway.

"I have heard talk of an exercise class being formed on Tuesday mornings after Mass, and I am pondering signing up for it." Abigail smiled. "Can't you just see Patrice and myself attempting jumping jacks!"

Clare laughed out loud. "Forgive me."

Abigail began to laugh too. "Now, child, add to that picture Sister Kathleen in her orthopedic shoes!"

They stopped walking as their laughter crescendoed down the hallway. Clare wiped tears from her eyes. Just when she thought she had regained her composure, a new wave of laughter came over her.

"Remember, you become faint if you laugh too hard."

"I'm all right." Clare tried to settle herself down. "I can't get that picture of Sister Kathleen out of my mind."

"My sides are aching." Abigail laughed again. "I think I am having a muscle cramp in my face." She let go of Clare's arm and rubbed her cheeks with her hands. "There—all right. Yes, that's much better. We greatly needed such a gift of laughter, but now we must be on our way."

The two nuns resumed their trip. Abigail leaned heavily on Clare as they turned into the hallway leading to the visiting area and to Sister Janice's desk.

"Good morning, Sister Abigail," Sister Janice said. "What can I do for you?"

"I would like to place a call to my convent."

"Didn't Clare tell you? I already called. Something must be wrong with the lines."

"Please," said Abigail with patience. "Could you try once more?"

Sister Janice opened a large binder and flipped through the pages until she reached one containing Abigail's name. Clare looked down to see the phone number of the Sisters of the Divine Name convent written across the top in blue ink, and dozens of entries neatly recorded in pencil on the lines below.

The young nun picked up the phone and dialed the numbers with the eraser end of a pencil. "Ringing—ringing. I know this is frustrating for you, Sister Abigail, but I'm sure whatever is causing the problem will be cleared up soon."

"But I would like for soon to be now."

Sister Janice cleared the phone line. "Let me try again." She dialed the number. "Ringing, ringing."

Abigail waited another moment. "Thank you for your efforts, Sister."

"I don't mind letting it ring."

"I have taken enough of your time," she said, giving Clare's arm a gentle squeeze. "We will be on our way."

Clare led Abigail past the visiting area. "I saw something," she whispered.

"And I heard something. . . . Are we near the sanctuary?"

"The door is right here, on your left."

"Let's go inside where our privacy is assured."

The two nuns moved into a pew. After she sat down, Clare leaned over and whispered, "What did you hear?"

"She never completed the call. I heard ten taps both times, and there should be eleven. There is the 1 at the beginning, plus three for the area code, plus seven for the number, which totals eleven, but I heard only ten taps."

"I watched her place both calls."

"And what did you see?"

"She is leaving off the last number, the nine."

Abigail frowned. "Now I am certain that her actions are deliberate. That phone could not have been ringing with only ten numbers dialed." She thought for a moment. "What time is it?"

"I don't know, nine-thirty, ten perhaps."

"I think I will attempt a call of my own."

Clare got up. "I'll take you."

She led Abigail across the hall and into the dining room. "This is disobedience, child. Wait for me here. I will not let you travel on this path."

Clare continued to walk. "You were told not to attempt calls except through Sister Janice. I was not."

"Good, then I will be spared the frustration of trying to locate the correct buttons."

Clare stopped in front of the wall-mounted phone. She lifted the receiver and handed it to Abigail. "Can you hear the dial tone?"

"Yes—I hear it."

"I push *0* for the operator."

"It's not ringing," Abigail said worriedly.

"Let me start again." Clare cleared the line. "Do you hear the dial tone?"

"I do. Please, try to hurry before we are discovered."

"It should be ringing."

"It is," Abigail said excitedly. "Yes operator, I would like to place a collect phone call to—"

"Sister Abigail!" said Sister Eva with frustration. "Hang up that phone." With a brisk walk she came over and stood in front of the elderly women. "Mother Francesca will be very disappointed with you."

Abigail handed the phone over to Clare and asked, "How is it that whenever I pick up this phone someone comes rushing in?"

"Look here," Sister Eva said as she picked up the phone. "Do you see the small triangle beside where it says line three?"

"My eyes fail me, Sister," Abigail answered. "I see no triangle."

"I see it," Clare said.

"We have four phone lines at Tranquil Garden. Lines one and two serve the nurses' stations and the staff offices, line four serves the Critical Care Unit, and line three serves the kitchen staff. Whenever the phone is in use that triangle can be seen from any other phone. That line is watched closely—it has to be." Sister Eva took the phone from Clare and hung it up. "You would be surprised how many people will make a long distance call at our expense."

"But as I explained to Sister Judith, I am making a collect call," Abigail protested.

"Mother Francesca wants you to make your calls the same way everyone else does." Abigail's face fell. "I'm sorry—I really am," said Sister Eva. "But Mother was very specific about her wishes."

"I understand," Abigail conceded.

"Can I get a wheelchair and take you back to your room?"

Abigail turned away. "No, thank you."

"We will find another way to reach your convent," Clare said as their steps inched along slowly.

"Now that I am aware of the reasons for the failures of my previous attempts, I believe the path has been made clearer. I think I know how to get through to my community. Certainly our friendly phone monitors can not always be present. I will wait for the Lord to provide an opportunity to place a call at a more unexpected hour."

Twenty-One

Outside the windows of room 142, lightning flashed. It was not the late-night storm, though, that caused Clare to lie on her bed with her eyes open. She was waiting.

Once the height of the storm passed, she sat up and threw off the covers. She searched the floor with sock-covered feet for her fuzzy white slippers as she retrieved her robe from the bedpost.

Her eyes slowly adjusted to the brightness of the hallway as she walked to an exit on the south side of the building. She stepped outside. The wind no longer howled. Distant thunder echoed off the walls. The intensity of the falling rain eased.

She had two choices: a stone staircase to the left; a longer, muddier trail to the right; both led to the bottom of the retaining wall. She took off her slick-bottomed slippers and headed toward the left.

The wet stones felt cold to her bare feet as she descended the stairs.

"Help me!" a woman cried in a thin, fearful voice.

Clare rushed toward the sound as the moon's light burst through the breaking clouds. She knelt down. Within seconds, her robe and gown were soaked in a puddle of chilled rainwater, sending uncontrollable shivers through her body. Yet she gathered herself enough to speak. "Don't be afraid, Gloria. I'm here."

"Clare?"

She reached for the fallen woman's hand. "Yes."

"How did you know?" she asked weakly.

"The Lord summoned me."

"It's—it's too late to stop my death. Too much has been broken within me." She gripped Clare's hand. "This is nearly unbearable pain—my insides are burning."

Clare looked up. A flash of lightning gave her a better view of the thirty feet to the top of the retaining wall. "It will be soon."

"They killed Florence and in—in a few more moments they will have succeeded in killing me. You—you are next, Clare."

"Yes, I know," she said, stroking Gloria's hand.

"Leave this place before it is too late!" said Gloria, putting her whole body's strength into the warning.

In a soothing voice Clare said, "Nothing is

going to happen to me that hasn't been ordained by God's mighty hand."

"They intend to kill you."

"And if they succeed I will gain the joys of heaven a little sooner. Be at peace about me."

Gloria moaned softly. "I can see something."

Clare looked toward the water. "Tell me what you see."

"A deep canyon. Can you see it just beyond the shore? Small rocks with more brilliance than diamonds line the sides. I see a light radiating above the canyon. It shines as bright as a thousand suns."

"How beautiful."

A trail of blood flowed down the side of Gloria's mouth. "Do you see it?"

"It's not for me to see, not yet."

"He is waiting for me." Gloria closed her eyes. "Soon I will see Him."

Clare wiped the rain from Gloria's face as she breathed her last.

As she returned to room 142, Clare found that the walk seemed long, her legs seemed heavy. She found her roommate sitting up in bed and the lights on. "Abigail, you should be asleep."

"My heart was troubled."

Clare approached Abigail's bed. "Should I call the nurse?"

"Prayer was the medication called for. And now that your expedition is over I am no longer troubled. It would be reasonable to assume that you were again out on one of your expeditions?"

"It would," Clare said as she removed her wet robe. "I am grateful for your prayers."

Abigail straightened her pillows and lay back down. "Who is no longer among us?"

"Gloria."

In a serious tone, Abigail asked, "Was the death a natural occurrence?"

Clare switched off the lamp and pulled the covers up around her neck. "No, Abigail, it was not."

Twenty-Two

The serving line emptied as the dining room reached full capacity. The sounds of plates and cups being unloaded filled the spacious room, as did the voices of the nuns eager to share whatever bits of information they managed to gather overnight concerning Sister Gloria's death. It had been two days since the gruesome discovery, and, just as with the death of Sister Florence, there were more questions than answers.

Sister Janice made her way to the center of the dining room as forks and spoons clanged their strange music. "Sisters, if I may have your attention." The room quieted. "As acting interim director of the Tranquil Garden Nursing Home, I must announce a disheartening situation. We have discovered numerous discrepancies in billing invoices over the past several months that could not be resolved to our satisfaction. Because we are seeking to be good stewards of God's financial blessings, we are now looking for a new distributor. Until that process is complete, we ask your patience for any food shortages we may incur. Thank you, Sisters."

Sister Kathleen asked, "I wonder what kind of shortages they're expecting?"

Abigail dragged her spoon along the bottom of her oatmeal bowl. "I can easily do without anything except this delightful maple syrup."

"I hope it isn't apricots," Monica said. "I love their chilled apricots."

"You don't want to be around me in the morning if I haven't had a cup of coffee," Sister Kathleen said.

"I'm content as long as I get a dessert with my dinner," Patrice said. "I'm not particular about what kind of dessert as long as I get one."

Clare held up a strip of bacon. "I do like to start out the day with breakfast meats."

Graciella held up a small crust. "I like toast."

Sister Kathleen looked over her glasses at Graciella. "Morning after morning we watch you eat your two slices of dry toast—and it isn't part of a spiritual discipline?"

Graciella smiled, then shook her head. "I just like toast."

As she put her fork down, Sister Kathleen said, "Maybe Sister Graciella's breakfast is the right one this morning."

"What do you mean?" Patrice asked.

"I just don't see how anyone can eat at a time like this. Sister Gloria is found dead at the bottom of the retaining wall, and no one can explain what happened. I can't eat a thing."

Monica poked at her eggs. "What was she doing outside in the storm?"

"And how did she get that wheelchair *to* the retaining wall, not to mention get herself *over* it?" added Sister Kathleen. "There's no sidewalk in that direction."

"She didn't get to the retaining wall *or* over it on her own," said Monica. "Gloria was killed, killed by a depraved soul."

"Nothing has been proven," Patrice said.

"Not that I want to, but I believe Monica," Sister Kathleen said. "If she says it's evil, I believe her."

"Yes, Monica has a sensitive spirit," agreed Abigail. "And I, too, believe her."

"Look, Sister Janice is coming back to tell us something," Patrice said, "and Mother Francesca is with her—another big announcement, I suppose."

"Tranquil Garden is becoming entirely too stressful," said Sister Kathleen as she scanned the room. "I wonder what's going on now?"

"I apologize for interrupting your breakfast a second time," Sister Janice said, "but we have some news that you should all hear." She turned to her superior. "Mother."

"There are rumors circulating concerning the recent death of Sister Gloria. These can be addressed at this time." Mother Francesca waited for the room to become completely silent. "The unthinkable has happened here at Tranquil Garden. The coroner has ruled Sister Gloria's death a suicide."

The hum of whispers filled the air. "I know it is a terrible shock," she continued. "We are faced with many challenges as we age. The loss of friends and loved ones and the deterioration of our health often leads to depression. Sister Gloria suffered from a number of maladies that affect many of us, but she was also devastated after recently leaving behind the convent where she had lived since her nineteenth birthday. It proved to be too much for her."

Mother Francesca looked with compassion into the faces of those near her. "We don't want this tragedy repeated, Sisters. We urge you to come to us if the frustration of aging becomes overwhelming. Our purpose here at Tranquil Garden is to help you through any difficult days you may have. We can not do that without your cooperation. We can not get you the help you need if we are not aware of the problem. I urge you to let us minister to all of your needs. That is what we are here for." She paused a moment. "Are there any questions?"

"Will there be a memorial service?"

"Yes, tomorrow evening at seven o'clock."

She waited for a moment. "Now Sisters, I will let you return to your breakfast."

Sister Kathleen picked up her water glass. "Seventy years of religious life and Sister Gloria forsakes her divine calling over arthritis? I don't believe it. Arthritis is painful, but landing at the bottom of the retaining wall couldn't have been any more pleasant—now, if she had saved up her heart medicine . . ."

Monica put her hands to her ears. "Don't harbor such thoughts. It is not for us to decide when life ends."

"Gloria did not kill herself," Abigail said with conviction. "I visited her the day she died, and I can assure you she had no intention of committing suicide."

"But a coroner said she did," Patrice said, "and he should know."

Abigail put her spoon into her empty bowl. "On the day of her death she was concerned both for her own life and the life of another Sister."

"*Concerned* as in thinking her life would be threatened?" Monica asked.

"Sister Clare," Sister Kathleen said, "didn't Sister Gloria arrive when you did?"

Clare nodded. "We are from the same community."

"Florence was also a Sister of the Sacred Heart," said Abigail.

Tapping the table for emphasis, Sister Kathleen said, "And both Gloria and Florence died under pretty strange circumstances, if you ask me."

Sister Kathleen sat quietly while she stared curiously at Clare. "She was concerned about the life of another Sister. Three Sisters of the Sacred Heart came into Tranquil Garden, and now two of them are dead."

The table became silent. Clare lowered her napkin. "I am the one Gloria was concerned about."

"Why would anyone want to kill three old nuns from the Sisters of the Sacred Heart?" Sister Kathleen asked.

"It doesn't make sense," Abigail said.

Monica looked at Clare. "You don't seem concerned."

"All things are in His mighty hands—be at peace about me, all of you."

Sister Kathleen picked up her water glass again. "Well, I think something really strange is going on here. First Sister Florence takes a deadly fall down a flight of stairs, then the driver of Sister Emily's taxi gets a lethal dose of heart medicine by mistake, and now Sister Gloria somehow manages to get a wheelchair to the retaining wall so she can jump out." She leaned forward. "If I were Sister Clare, I think I would stay away from high places."

Twenty-Three

Is that another letter?" asked Clare as she sat down in her chair.

"Sister Janice brought it by while you were gone." Abigail handed it to her. "Will you read it to me?"

"It has a Freeport postmark."

"That does not come to me as a surprise, but we may still find it of some interest."

Clare tore open the envelope and unfolded the letter.

> *"To our dearest Abigail. As the days of separation draw to a close we look forward to your return to us. We know that these final weeks will pass quickly. All of the Sisters send along their prayers and ask that you continue to pray for their intentions—"*

"I have heard enough." Abigail adjusted her glasses. "If you will put it with the others."

Clare walked over to the night table and

opened the drawer. "We should be on our way to the dining room."

"Is it already time for dinner?" Abigail sighed. "I seem to have lost my appetite. If I only understood the actions that are taking place; if only the Lord would reveal to me why He is allowing this isolation from my community. Sister Janice told Emily that my community was no longer sending letters. What if that is true, and Sister Janice really is trying to shield my heart from the pain of abandonment?"

"How long have you been in community?"

"For too many years to count."

"And after all of those years, do you truly think they would abandon you?" Abigail shook her head. "You will get through to your convent," Clare assured.

"But not today."

"No," Clare agreed. "Not today."

Abigail pushed herself up from her chair. "Here I am indulging my prideful self once again. Hardship isn't mine alone within these walls."

"Nor will it ever be. The condition of life knows no strangers."

Abigail took Clare's arm. The women walked with their usual lack of speed down the east wing, then turned into east/west hallway leading to the dining room. The sound of shuffling feet echoed from the tile floor and grew louder as other nuns from other sections of the nursing home converged for the evening meal.

Clare felt someone tap on her shoulder. She looked to her left and smiled. Graciella stood there.

"Shall we pray, dear one?" asked Graciella.

Clare nodded. "I would like that." She turned to Abigail. "We are going to the sanctuary for prayer—join us."

Abigail let go of Clare's arm. "All of this walking has brought back my appetite. You two go on, and say a prayer for me. Say several prayers."

Graciella led the way into the sanctuary and selected a pew about midway to the altar.

"I received a letter today," Graciella said. "Telling me that my youngest sister has gone on to be with the Lord. For six years she battled cancer, underwent every treatment. Nothing helped."

"She is at peace now."

"I will follow her shortly." She smiled at Clare. "Cancer first struck my body three years ago. Last December, it returned."

"Is there a treatment?"

"Not one I intend to take, dear one." She looked at the life-sized crucifix mounted on the wall behind the altar. "My earthly service will soon end, but my eternal service began many, many years ago." Smiling, she continued. "I had no interest in the games other children played. You?" Clare shook her head. "My brothers and sisters teased me considerably. So, as often as I could, I ran off to the only place I could be alone."

"The church," said Clare.

"I would slip inside and sit until the parish priest chased me away. Once I went in and lay down in order to avoid being seen. While I lay there, I fell asleep, and I had the most wonderful dream."

"Tell me your dream."

"I saw a man walking in a beautiful meadow. I followed him over to a single tree. He sat on the ground beside this tree and rested beneath its branches. For some time I watched him. He continued to rest against the tree for what seemed like hours; then he leaned forward, and I saw that the bark on the tree had been rubbed smooth where the man's shoulder had been touching the tree."

"It was a tree the man visited often."

"Yes. To me it was a symbol of prayer."

Clare needed no further explanation. The women sat in silence for more than an hour. Neither struggled against the distracting thoughts that occasionally visited, and neither struggled against their time of prayer coming to an end.

"I am going on, dear one," Graciella said as she got up from the pew.

Clare turned to get her legs out of the way and allow Graciella to pass more easily. "Sleep well, Sister."

Another hour passed before Clare got up and returned to her room. She found Abigail sitting in her chair, seemingly deep in thought. Though Clare made a special effort to become situated without distracting her roommate, the chair made an unusual squeak as she sat down.

"Are you hungry?" Abigail asked.

"It can wait until morning."

"Monica and Patrice donated their dinner rolls to you. I wrapped them in a napkin and put them in my pocket. Would you like to have them?"

"I would."

Abigail put her hand into the pocket of her habit. "I would have donated my roll, but I ended up being very hungry." She pulled out a bundle wrapped in white linen. "I ate mine."

Clare smiled as she reached for the bundle. "Thank you for making the delivery."

"You missed a good dinner except for the green beans. They came from a can and tasted like metal." Abigail made a face. "I can tell a canned vegetable on the very first bite."

"I thought they pride themselves on serving only fresh vegetables here."

"They usually do, but until a new food distributor is arranged, we will have to tolerate some canned foods. I found out the spinach was fresh only after completing my turn through the serving line, so tomorrow night I will ask for that."

Clare sat next to Abigail and began eating a roll. Abigail leaned closer to her and breathed deeply. "Heaven's aroma flows from you." Then Abigail's eyes opened wide. "It's a smell I know well. Can it be? Give me your hand." Clare offered her right hand. Abigail smelled her hand, breathing deeply again. Then she let Clare's hand go. "Tell me, child, what color are your eyes?"

"They are blue."

Abigail adjusted her glasses. "And do they have flecks of gray within them?"

"They do."

"And would it be reasonable to assume that you belonged to a community before joining the Sisters of the Sacred Heart?"

"It would."

"And it would be reasonable to assume that your last name is Aames, and that before your profession to the Sisters of the Sacred Heart, your first name was Rachel?"

"Yes," Clare answered softly. "My name was Rachel, and yes, I was once a novice in the Sisters of the Divine Name community."

"You know who I am, child?"

"Yes."

Abigail's voice shook with emotion. "Is there anything you would like to say to me?"

"There is."

Abigail's face stiffened as if she were expecting a heavy blow. "Then speak your mind."

Clare reached out her hand and placed it on Abigail's arm. "I've missed you."

At hearing the response, a tear fell from Abigail's eye. "And I have missed you. Why didn't you tell me who you were?"

"You said you wanted to guess."

"That I did." Abigail took Clare's hand into her own. "This revelation is not the great surprise it should be. I knew from the beginning that we knew each other." She took a long breath. "I knew the powers of darkness had sent their laborers to this place the day I arrived in late October, but I had no idea for what purpose. And here you were all along as the story unfolded." She covered her mouth with her hand. "This means you are in grave danger, child. We must find a way to get you out of here."

"My community will not remove me from this place."

"And if we found a way to go to the authorities, I suspect they would consider us to be suffering from dementia." Abigail thought for a moment. "The answer lies in restoring communication to my community. They alone would accept our testimony. But my every attempt to reach them has failed."

Clare set her dinner roll down on the linen napkin. "He is ever faithful."

"You believe His word will be fulfilled and The Order will be restored."

"Yes."

"I hear such confidence, but the question ringing in my ears is how?"

"If it is ours to know, we will know; otherwise we must trust that not knowing is the better way."

They reflected for a moment, then Abigail said, "I asked if there was anything you would like to say to me. But now I would like to say something to you." Abigail cleared her throat gently. "I am truly sorry."

"There is nothing to be sorry for."

"Indeed, there is."

Clare shook her head. "Indeed, there is not."

Twenty-Four

Abigail earnestly searched the hallway for any vague form that might be identified as Patrice. At long last she made out a blur that could belong to no one else.

"Good afternoon, Patrice," Abigail said. "If you will close the door, we are ready to begin."

"Why close the door?" asked Sister Kathleen. "Sister Abigail—Sister Patrice, what are you doing? We never make rosaries with the door closed."

"Abigail told me to close it."

"Is something wrong?" asked Monica.

"Only that I have something to tell you today that must be kept confidential." Abigail came to the table. "Today is a day of revelation, Sisters." She sat herself down carefully. "Just as our dear Graciella so wisely directed, it was not our task to go about locating Novice Rachel. The Lord Himself has revealed her whereabouts."

"You know where Novice Rachel is?" Monica asked.

"I do, and I can assure you that she is not tending to grandchildren on a front porch in Florida or anywhere else."

Sister Kathleen leaned forward on one elbow and looked over her glasses. "So where is she?"

"She is right here at Tranquil Garden, and I would like you all to meet her."

Monica looked up. "We would be honored, Abigail. When can we meet her?"

Abigail smiled mischievously. "I was thinking you should meet her right now."

"What's going on here?" Sister Kathleen asked as she tapped her pliers on the table surface. "Something is going on—that look your face—it's Graciella," she said with certainty. "Graciella is Novice Rachel."

"I am not the dear one," Graciella stated simply.

"Dear one," Monica repeated. She looked across the table. "That is what Graciella calls Clare."

"Somebody better explain things," Sister Kathleen said.

Clare looked at each of the Sisters and said, "Before my profession into the Sisters of the Sacred Heart, my Baptismal name was Rachel Aames."

"I knew it," Sister Kathleen said with conviction. "I knew it all along."

"There is one more revelation to be made,

Sisters," said Abigail in a serious tone. "During the year that Clare was a novice with the Sisters of the Divine Name, I held the office of Mistress of Novices."

"Mercy sakes! You were the one—" Sister Kathleen said, "you were the one who—"

"Yes, who brought devastation to an entire community through the fault of pride. It is true. I am the one who selected Sister Theresa. And I am the one who remained silent when it was clear that a mistake had been made."

"You were called Mother Abigail?" Monica asked. "I always wanted to be called Mother Monica."

"Actually," Clare said. "We didn't call her Mother Abigail, we called her—"

"Say no more, child," Abigail interrupted. "They will only tease me and think it is silly. I held that name quite dear and will not have it giggled over."

"We wouldn't," Monica insisted.

"Well, I might," Patrice said. "Just tell us."

"I believe it was a take-off of sorts of her Christian name," Clare offered.

Sister Kathleen asked, "What was your Christian name?"

Abigail hesitated. "It was Elizabeth."

Patrice counted on her fingers. "Mother Lizzy, Mother Liz, Mother Beth."

"No, no, and no. Now, enough of this. It is

not a name you will guess, and as honored as I am that you will all still sit at the same table with me despite the knowledge of my many failings in giving service to Our Lord, there is still much to discuss."

"We all make mistakes, Abigail," Monica soothed. "Big ones."

"I never made any that big," Sister Kathleen said quietly.

"Hush, Sister Kathleen," Patrice scolded.

"I am sure none of you did, but this day of revelation is not about my many failings. This day is about His redemptive power to restore whatever is His."

"But The Order," said Monica with hesitation. "How can The Order be restored if Clare didn't receive the laying on of hands and hear the words of the sacred prayer?"

"And what about the ancient question?" Sister Kathleen asked. "Somebody would have had to answer it."

"True," said Abigail as she turned and looked at Clare. "I would like those answers myself."

Clare put her pliers down. "The divine summons came in the middle of the night. The Lord already prepared my heart for a ministry to the dying, so I assumed that was His purpose.

"As I entered the Room of Waiting, the power of God was too strong for me. I knelt beside Sister Dominique's bed, aware that she had something to tell me, aware that she was engaged in an intense personal spiritual battle. I felt unworthy to be at her bedside and bowed my head low. Ever so gently I was made to understand another purpose for this visit. I told her of a vision and she proposed a question. When I answered, she passed the mantle of graces on to me.

"After that, Sister Dominique became calm, in a state of waiting. I'm sure she thought I had gone, but I sat with her until the Lord took her from this life."

"God's protection prevailed." Abigail rubbed her forehead. "The mantle did not pass when I escorted Sister Theresa into the chamber. I didn't know."

"We have to get Clare back to your Motherhouse, Abigail," Monica said with urgency.

"That will be no easy task," Abigail said. "The situation is critical. Not only is all communication with my convent thwarted, but I am convinced Clare's life is in danger. You must know that both Florence and Gloria's deaths were intentional."

"There's enough suspicion around to convince me," Sister Kathleen said.

"I can not give you the evidence required for a court of law, but I can tell you from experience, from living through this nightmare more than fifty years ago, that the powers of darkness are involved here."

"Through whose hands?" asked Monica, her voice shaking.

"It may be through more than one set of hands. It's as if Sister Theresa were at work again."

"And she is," Graciella announced. "Sister Theresa is here."

Abigail's face paled.

"Abigail," Clare called from across the table. She left her chair and went to Abigail's side. "Are you all right?"

"Who, Graciella," Abigail said weakly. "Do you know who she is?"

"I do not."

"We can figure this out," Sister Kathleen insisted. "Abigail, what did she look like?"

"After so many years, any description I could give would be considerably invalid. She could be any of the nuns in any of these rooms. This explains many things."

"Does it?" Monica asked.

"Oh yes, it explains why all my letters from the Motherhouse have disappeared, and why I have received a sham set of letters that my Sisters never wrote. It explains why my phone calls to the community never went through. Why Clare was kept from seeing Gloria, while I was allowed easy access. Why deadly coffee was delivered to that taxi driver. I am certain these incidents, as well as the deaths of Florence and Gloria, are all the work of the evil one through Sister Theresa."

"She intends to kill Clare?" Patrice asked.

"Somehow it was known that one of the three nuns who arrived here from the Sisters of the Sacred Heart was the lost member of The Order, and yes, the intention must be to kill all three, ensuring victory for the powers of darkness."

"I think I know who she is," Sister Kathleen said. All eyes turned to her. "Those young Sisters of Mercy are always in the room next to ours with Sister Joanne, but she almost never comes out."

"I'm sure this is gossip," Monica said regretfully, "but she always has her meals in her room."

"Which is against the rules," Sister Kathleen pointed out. "To maintain ambulatory status a resident must receive her meals in the dining room."

Abigail reached for another bead. "Speculation can not concern us at this time. We must concentrate our energies on getting Clare safely away from this place. I must get through to the Sisters of the Divine Name."

"One of us could call your community," Monica offered. "We could send word for you."

"Sister Janice sits right on top of the phone," Sister Kathleen complained. "There's no way to make a private call from her desk. We could try to make a call from another phone."

"Clare and I have made several attempts without success."

"I could write a letter," Patrice said slowly. "I could write a letter to my community with a letter addressed to yours inside. Then, when my letter arrives, one of the Sisters from my community can mail off the one to the Sisters of the Divine Name."

"That could work," Clare said.

"Yes, each of you send a letter telling my community that Novice Rachel has been found—but do not mention Clare's name in case your letters are opened."

"But they can't open our letters," Patrice said.

Sister Kathleen looked at Patrice over her glasses. "They have pushed an elderly nun down a staircase and another one over a retaining wall; opening your mail wouldn't be a cause for any loss of sleep, I'm sure."

"We must be very cautious in the days to come, Sisters," Abigail said. "Speak of this to no one, and pray with all your might."

Sister Kathleen looked around the room. "Sister Theresa is really here at Tranquil Garden?"

"What community would have taken her?" Monica asked.

"Any community," Abigail answered. "Sister Theresa had every appearance of being a normal, balanced, well-meaning, and kind-hearted woman. Securing a vocation to any convent would not have been out of the question by any means. In our community the novitiate lasted two years, which meant Sister Theresa had not taken first vows. There had been no notation made to her baptismal certificate. There was no record that she had been with the Sisters of the Divine Name."

Sister Kathleen shuddered. "Then she could have joined any community without their knowing about her spiritual lapse in the prayer chamber and her visit to the asylum?"

"It appears that is precisely what she did," Abigail said.

Patrice hunted for a bead. "Well, I'm not going to get much sleep knowing Sister Theresa could be my roommate."

"Me either," Monica confessed.

"Mercy sakes, Monica," Sister Kathleen said with frustration. "I'm your roommate and I guarantee each of you I am not Sister Theresa."

"I'm sorry, I didn't mean *you* could be. I'm just very concerned."

"Don't be concerned," Clare said gently. "In the end, all will be as God wills."

Monica studied Clare for a moment. "You're not afraid?"

Clare shook her head. "There is nothing to be afraid of."

"Getting too much help going down a flight of stairs is something to be afraid of, if you ask me," Sister Kathleen said.

Abigail moved her beads aside. "Let us put away our rosaries for the moment. We have letters to write and place in the mail today. Remember, Sisters, to remind them that all communications by phone or letter have failed. Ask them to please send someone here to Tranquil Garden right away." Abigail adjusted her glasses.

"From here we will have to walk by faith alone. Pray, Sisters, that one of these letters gets through in time. For The Order to be restored, Clare must be removed from the danger that surrounds her."

Twenty-Five

Before the first hints of sunlight broke out over the horizon, Clare heard the sound of Abigail moving around in their room.

"Where are you going?" Clare asked as she sat up in bed.

"Go back to sleep, child," Abigail instructed. "I will not risk your being discovered on this mission of mine. Stay behind and offer prayer during my absence. We are in need of some success."

Abigail opened the door to the hallway and began her journey. She gripped the handrail for assurance as she slowly progressed up the hallway. Her black, soft-soled shoes gained a few inches with each silent step. She turned right into the east/west hallway, then left into the dining room. As the excitement of nearing her destination increased, she found it harder to maintain her breath. She moved around the serving counter and felt along the lightly textured wall. Locating the phone, she counted the small plastic squares until reaching the ninth button, and pushed it firmly. The dial tone buzzed in her ear. She counted again and pushed the first button on the fourth row. Nothing happened. She pushed it again, and again nothing happened.

"Morning, Sister Abigail," Robert said as he came out the swinging door separating the kitchen from the dining room. "You're a bit early for breakfast. I don't even have the water up for the oatmeal yet."

"I am not here for my morning meal. I was making a call, but the phone is broken."

He set a box down. "I had to drive forty miles to get this case of nonfat creamer. The store in town is loaded with only the regular kind."

"How can they have cream without fat?" Abigail asked. "I don't think it would still be cream, do you?"

"I guess it's more chemicals and fillers than cream. The doctors are big on no-fat everything, but if you ask me, I think we're all better off with the real thing."

"I agree."

"So—this thing is broken?"

Abigail handed him the handset. "I push the button and it does nothing."

"But you have to push more than one button."

"I am calling the operator, so I only need to

dial 9 to get an outside line, and 0 to get the operator."

"And it won't do that?" Robert cleared the line and returned the receiver. "Here—try again."

Abigail pushed 9. "There is the tone for the outside line." She pushed the first button on the fourth row. "Again—nothing."

"I see what's wrong." Robert took hold of the old woman's finger and raised it to the buttons. "The 0 is the middle button on the bottom row—you were pushing the star button."

"The star button," Abigail repeated with amusement. "Our convent still has a rotary phone. Dialing was only 0 through 9."

"It's used with automated phone systems," he said in response to her confused expression. "Businesses use them. It's kind of complicated." He cleared the line again. "Try again, Sister."

Abigail pushed 9, then the middle button on the fourth row. "Yes, operator—I would like to make a collect call. Yes, I have the phone number."

Robert looked up. "Good morning, Mother Francesca."

"What is going on here?" she asked.

"Abigail is making a call."

"What is our policy on using this phone, Robert?"

"It's all right, she's calling collect."

"It is not all right," Mother Francesca said with authority. "Abigail, hang up that phone."

Abigail cupped her hand over the receiver. "This is Abigail," she said frantically. "Do not hang up."

"I told you to hang up that phone."

"I will not."

Mother Francesca looked calmly at Robert. "You may return to your duties in the kitchen."

She waited until he left the room. "Hang up the phone."

"I will not. I have finally reached my convent and I will speak to them."

"You can speak to them through the proper channels once Sister Janice arrives at nine o'clock."

"The calls that she places for me can never go through," Abigail explained tiredly. "She is not dialing all of the numbers."

"Of course she is."

"She is not," Abigail said strongly. "And she is not mailing my letters, and she is sending me letters from my convent that she actually writes herself."

"That's impossible," Mother Francesca argued. "Sister Janice would never do such things—you must be mistaken."

"Check the postmarks on the letters in the drawer of my night table yourself. You will find only Freeport and Houston postmarks on the envelopes."

"Give me the phone."

"No."

"This disobedience doesn't suit you. Give me the phone."

Abigail handed her the receiver. "Hello? Yes, this is Mother Francesca from the Tranquil Garden Nursing Home. Actually, I am a bit confused at the moment, who may I speak to regarding Abigail?" She put her hand over the phone. "They are bringing Sister Alicia to the phone."

"May I please speak to her?"

Mother Francesca raised her hand and signaled for silence. "I am well, thank you. Yes, there seems to have been some sort of communications problem. . . . No, I am unaware of any illness, Sister Abigail is just fine." A moment passed. "She has not received correspondence from you either, and there has been some problem with getting through by phone. You are of course welcome to visit at any time. . . . You were told what? I see. When do you think you will be coming? . . . Yes, if you will call me back when I am at my desk, we can make the final arrangements. She is right here. Certainly, and I will get to the source of these mix-ups immediately." Mother Francesca lowered the phone to Abigail. "Here you are."

"I'm here," Abigail said softly. The old woman's tear-filled eyes closed as she listened to the voice on the other end. "Tell me that I will not wake up from a dream. Tell me it is really you, child."

"I'm really here, Mother," Alicia soothed. "I will bring the words of the final prophecy as soon as I can arrange a flight."

Abigail smiled. "Another messenger has already made the delivery."

"Were you given an interpretation?"

"I was, but it will have to wait for another time."

"You can not speak freely."

"That is correct."

"We were told you were ill. Now I am told you are not. I'm concerned."

"As you should be."

"Then something *is* wrong."

"Yes, the weather is wonderful."

"I will get there as quickly as I can," Alicia promised. "I will see you in a few days."

Abigail handed the phone over to Mother Francesca. "I ask your forgiveness for my disobedience."

"All is forgotten," she said. "It looks as if you will be having a visitor soon."

"Indeed—the hours will seems like days."

"I hope that you will forgive the inconveniences that you have suffered."

Abigail adjusted her glasses. "What inconveniences? All is forgotten."

A pleased smile parted Mother Francesca's face. "Can I locate a wheelchair for you? There is still an hour before breakfast will be served."

"No, thank you, the walk will do me good."

"Very well then, I will excuse myself into the kitchen to ensure that Robert's feelings were not hurt by my earlier abruptness."

Abigail moved around the counter and negotiated through the open strip that separated two rows of tables. The sight of a white-haired nun in a worn linen habit inching her way along the blue-bordered tiles of the Tranquil Garden Nursing Home gave away no visible sign of the victory that had taken place. Her step held no triumphant bounce; her eyes held no hint of the relief in which she had been bathed.

"Good morning, Sister," Tom greeted.

"Will my passing through interfere with your work?"

"Not at all, you go right ahead." He watched her progress slowly down the hall, then he called out to her. "Could I ask you something, Sister?"

Abigail stopped walking. "Indeed you may."

Tom approached and placed his broom in front of him. Then he placed both hands on the handle and rested his chin on his hands. "I have a son. He's a grown man—on his own and all that. He went and got himself into some trouble. I've been praying about what to do. Wouldn't it be a sin to do nothing?"

"Has your son asked you to do anything?"

"No, Sister, I'm not even supposed to know about it."

"Has the Lord asked you to do anything?"

"No, Sister."

"Then doing nothing seems to be exactly what He wants you to do." Abigail smiled. "Be at peace. The trouble will bring your son no harm."

"It's as if God Himself is speaking through you." He studied her for a moment as the muscles in his neck and shoulders relaxed. "Thank you, Sister."

Abigail began to walk again. Her slow steps eventually led to room 142. "It's a glorious morning," she announced.

"It is," Clare agreed.

"I have news—wonderful news!"

"Your mission was a success!"

"On this beautiful Tuesday morning, I heard the sweet voice of one of the Sisters from my community."

"You finally managed to get through undiscovered?"

"No, I was discovered, but Mother Francesca allowed me to continue the call."

"Who did you get to speak with?"

"Sister Alicia, who tended to Sister Catherine in her final years. She has the manner of an angel and the ability to firmly command any situation. I have complete confidence that she will be able to arrange for you to accompany us when we hastily depart this place."

Clare closed the book she was reading. "When is she coming?"

"She will arrive at the first possible opportunity. She is aware of the urgency of this matter." Abigail leaned her head back and closed her eyes. "The Lord promised restoration of The Order, and so it will be. He has placed the plans for our rescue into motion. It will not be much longer."

Twenty-Six

Abigail situated her tray on the metal rails of the serving line.

"Morning, Sister Abigail," Robert said. "What can I get you today?"

"I will have a bowl of your delicious oatmeal. Go lightly on the butter, and be generous with the maple syrup."

"You know I can't do that today, Sister."

"And why is that?"

"Didn't one of the nurses explain to you that your blood work shows your sugar levels are too high? There's a danger of you developing diabetes. That means no syrup—and it means you'll probably have to take daily medications soon."

"I was told nothing about it."

"I'm sorry, Sister, but it's for your own good. Why don't you have some eggs this morning?"

"Very well." She received the plate and made her way to table nine.

Clare followed shortly after and unloaded her tray. "Eggs, Abigail?"

"It seems my phone call has not gone unnoticed—and this is the price." She pushed the plate away. "I can not eat them."

Clare pulled the plate toward her and set a bowl in front of Abigail. "Then perhaps you would like mine."

"Do I smell maple syrup?"

"Somewhere underneath it you will also find a serving of oatmeal."

Abigail reached for her spoon. "Bless you, child."

Monica and Sister Kathleen came to the table.

"This is why I don't like being the last one in line," said Sister Kathleen. "This pastry is hard as a rock."

"Graciella isn't joining us this morning?" Clare asked.

"I haven't seen her," Monica said.

Clare wiped her mouth. "Excuse me."

"Stay and eat," said Abigail. "You must keep up your strength."

Not wanting to correct her in front of others, Clare leaned over and whispered in the elder nun's ear, "Food alone will not do that."

Clare crossed the hallway and entered the sanctuary. She saw Graciella sitting in her usual pew near the front.

"May I join you?"

Graciella smiled.

The women prayed in silence until the breakfast hour was over.

"I will see you at lunch," Clare said.

"Wait." Graciella put her hand into the pocket of her habit. "I have something for you. I made it."

Clare took hold of the thick paper strip. "It's a bookmark. How lovely." She looked at the front. "He is ever faithful."

"You said it was your favorite saying."

"Yes, it is." She turned the card over, then back again. "Thank you so much."

Graciella smiled. "You are welcome, dear one."

"I first heard that saying from Abigail while I was in the novitiate of the Sisters of the Divine Name. One of the girls was an incessant worrier, and over and over again Abigail would soothe her with those words."

"It must have been a painful blow when your class was dismissed," Graciella said.

"It was a disappointment." She looked at the bookmark again. "But I knew I was called to live the consecrated life—it just would not be with that community. It was an uncertain time. It was then that those words first comforted my soul with a power soothing beyond every description. It was as if Jesus were singing them within my soul."

"Have you told Abigail this?"

"No, I haven't."

"She carries a burden from that age. One she unknowingly clutches and draws in on herself. Go—find Abigail and tell her of the comfort the words brought; it will release the guilt that grips her concerning you."

"Please excuse me." Clare left the chapel. She returned to room 142 and found it empty. Her blue eyes looked up. The clock on the wall reminded her that Abigail would be found in her usual spot on the wooden bench in the back courtyard. She left the room and made her way up the hallway to the door leading outside.

The warm gulf breeze and the smell coming from the citrus trees greeted her. She approached the wooden bench. "Would you mind if I joined you?"

"Indeed, I welcome the company." Abigail patted the spot next to her.

"I wanted to show you something." Clare placed the bookmark into Abigail's hand. "Graciella made it for me."

The elder nun looked at the thick strip of paper closely. "I am sure it is beautiful, but I am afraid I can not make out these words."

"It says, 'He is ever faithful.'"

Abigail smiled. "That reminds me of a novice—I can't recall her name. I repeated it to her often."

"Isadora," Clare answered.

"Indeed it was. You have a strong memory.

I didn't realize you were in the same novitiate class."

"I told Graciella during one of our first conversations in the chapel that it was my favorite saying. She remembered and made the bookmark for me."

"How could it be your favorite, when I—the most lowly of His creatures—was the origin of such a saying?"

Clare took hold of Abigail's hand. "I knew in those days that there was a great deal taking place that was not for me to understand. It was a difficult time. I was not at all eager to return to the world to start my vocational search from scratch, but it was done, and I was none the worse for wear."

"I abandoned you, child. I sent you off, knowing that you were of The Order. I sent you off questioning if you even had a vocation." Abigail lowered her head. "What kind of mother could do such a terrible thing to her child?"

"A mother who holds tremendous love for that child," Clare said softly. "Your actions saved lives."

"My actions protected my prideful and vain self. It was nothing less than pure selfishness. Had I gone to the Governess of The Order, the outcome would have been different."

Clare's voice became more intense. "If it were the outcome intended, the Lord would have seen to it that it took place despite whatever faults you held." She breathed deeply, then softly said, "Stop looking with the eyes of yesterday, and see with the eyes of the present."

"What do you mean, child?"

"He is—*ever faithful.* I cling to those words as much today as I did during those days of uncertainty. He is ever faithful; nothing has been lost."

"I kept you from the life you were to live within The Order."

"No," Clare disagreed. "My life has been exactly as it was supposed to be. And it has been a wondrous life. And this day that we are living now is exactly how it is supposed to be. It has been prophesied to be just as you saw in your vision."

"There is no regret in your voice, but is there any within your heart?"

"No, there is none."

Abigail raised trembling fingers and wiped tears from the side of her face. "Indeed, and from this hour forward there shall be none within mine." She squeezed Clare's hand firmly. "Soon, you will be safely within the grounds of the Sisters of the Divine Name. It is my prayer that once that work is complete, the Lord will see fit to dismiss this servant so that I might finally enjoy the bliss of divine union without the confines of this wearied body."

"And what if the Lord has other intentions?"

"He is a merciful God; certainly He will tire of my complaints and allow me permanent rest."

"Prepare yourself, Abigail—that type of rest may be some time off yet."

"Indeed, and what has the Lord revealed to you about His intentions for me?"

Clare smiled. "He will reveal it, and He will do so very soon."

"What is that over there, child?"

"That is Sister Kathleen coming out the door."

"It gave me a start." Abigail laughed. "I thought one of the trees sprang from the ground."

"Good afternoon, Sisters." She took a seat beside Clare. "What is so funny?"

"Nothing, dear," Abigail said.

"Then why were you both laughing while I was on my way over here?"

"Abigail thought you were a tree."

Sister Kathleen snickered. "Well, I never had a flattering figure, but I've never been mistaken for a tree." Her snicker grew into a full laugh, then faded as she spotted Monica walking past a window. "I've been thinking about what you told us at breakfast," she said. "With everything that's been going on here, I think

Sister Alicia should get all of us out of here, especially Sister Monica. She's just too delicate for all this. She was up with every creak this old building made last night. The poor woman is terrified, and I'm getting close to that myself."

"There will be no danger once Clare is gone," Abigail assured them. "We must begin praying for Alicia. If her heart is closed to my interpretation of the vision I received, I may be passed off as hysterical or accused of losing my mental faculties."

"You just tell her about the growing body count here at Tranquil Garden," Sister Kathleen said, "and I'm sure she'll pay attention."

"As with the situation fifty-eight years ago, nothing can be proven. I must remember to be cautious with my explanations."

Sister Kathleen shook her head. "I think you are putting yourself right from the frying pan into the fire by helping Clare. No offense, but what if this Sister Theresa, or whoever she is now, finds out you're planning Clare's escape? Mercy sakes, just look what happened to Emily—and all she was trying to do was get word to your convent."

"Be at peace," Abigail said softly. "Remember, we serve a powerful Lord, and He is ever faithful."

Twenty-Seven

Robert walked through the crowded terminal of Houston's William Hobby Airport. He didn't have much of a description of the woman he would be meeting and driving back to Tranquil Garden, but he reasoned he did not need much. A woman wearing any kind of religious habit in this day and age couldn't be that hard to find.

He walked up to a young woman wearing a white linen dress.

"Sister Alicia? My name is Robert Forrester. Sister Janice sent me over from the Tranquil Garden Nursing Home." He reached for her suitcase. "Please, let me take that."

"Thank you." She began walking beside him. "I want you to take me directly to Tranquil Garden."

"But I was told to take you to the guest quarters at the Sisters of Mercy convent first."

"I intend to see Abigail before doing anything else. I hope I have made myself clear?"

"Yes, Sister."

Robert led her to the cream-colored van. He opened the passenger door and closed it after she climbed inside. After loading her suitcase, he got in and turned on the engine, which needed a little coaxing. They headed away from the airport.

Sister Alicia sat, attentive and stiff, as she watched the passing street signs. "Why are we headed into Houston?" Robert did not answer. "The convent is the other way. We should be heading southeast."

Robert remained silent. The palms of her hands began to tingle as they would if she were standing in a high place. The light ahead was green. She reached for the door handle. The light turned yellow. Robert accelerated to beat the light, then pressed firmly on the brake.

"Why are we going into the city?"

The van slowed. Alicia looked at Robert. She looked at his eyes. He did not look like a madman—but then nothing about Tranquil Garden was what it appeared to be in these recent weeks.

She pulled on the handle.

"What are you doing, Sister?"

"You're going the wrong way."

"What was that?" Robert asked as he took a small earphone out of one ear. "I'm listening to a technology speech—awful stuff." He pointed to the van's cassette player. "I'd play it on that, but there's no use in both of us getting a headache."

"Why are we traveling north? Tranquil Garden is southwest."

"Only for a little further, Sister." Robert checked his rear-view mirror. "This road takes us to the South Freeway, which will take us down to Lake Jackson. Then we switch off to a little highway that takes us the rest of the way."

The light turned green.

Alicia pulled the door closed. "How long will this route take?"

"Forty-five minutes at the most." Robert turned his head. "Abigail is sure looking forward to seeing you."

"I've been trying to see her for weeks."

"Abigail is one of my favorites. Every morning she asks for the same thing. A bowl of oatmeal that's light on the butter and heavy on the warmed maple syrup."

Alicia smiled. "To her, maple syrup is a food group."

"Too bad about the diabetes. I'm sure it's hard on her not eating it anymore."

"Diabetes?"

"She doesn't have it yet, but her blood work's a little off. They don't want to take a chance."

"You're saying they no longer let her eat her favorite food because she might get diabetes?"

"Sounds like punishment when you say it like that," said Robert as he changed lanes. "You're really worried about her."

"First I'm told she's sick, then I'm told she's not, and now you say she might have diabetes."

"Well, I don't know who said she was sick, but I've seen her three mornings a week since she came back. She always has a smile and an appetite. She got a new roommate in January. Clare leads Abigail back and forth from the dining room like a doting daughter. They seem very fond of each other. You don't have anything to worry about. She's just fine."

Alicia looked out her window and Robert put his earphone back in his ear. The miles passed. The van pulled into the long driveway of the Tranquil Garden Nursing Home and parked in front of the fountain.

The sight of the massive structure caused Alicia to involuntarily shudder. Fear began to seize her as a thought echoed without welcome in her mind. Without realizing the words were leaving her mouth, she said, "Her compliance with evil is total."

"What did you say, Sister?"

"Nothing," said Alicia as she quickly opened her door. "I must get to Abigail."

"May I help you?" Sister Janice asked politely.

"I am here to see Abigail."

"You must be Sister Alicia. Welcome to Tranquil Garden. We weren't expecting you until later." She looked over the nun's shoulder. "Robert, weren't you supposed to take Sister Alicia to the convent first?"

"Is there a problem with my being here?"

"None whatsoever."

"Then if you will excuse me . . ."

"Don't you want to get settled at the convent first?"

"No. I want to see Abigail—now."

"Without delay." Sister Janice lowered her eyes. "Please wait here, Robert, we will only be a few minutes. This way, Sister." She led Alicia through the main entrance and motioned to the left. "If you will have a seat in our visiting area, I will bring Abigail at once."

"I would prefer to see her in her room," said Alicia firmly. "Is that a problem?"

"Most certainly not. This way." She led Sister Alicia through the visiting area and into the hallway. "I am especially glad you are here. We've been particularly worried about her lately."

"Didn't you tell me your name was Sister Bridgett?"

Sister Janice turned her head. "Have we spoken before?"

"You don't recognize my voice?" Sister Janice looked at her blankly. "I recognize yours. We must have spoken over the phone more than a dozen times during Abigail's illness."

"But Abigail hasn't been ill—and there is no Sister Bridgett here. You must be mistaken."

"I don't think so." Her face flushed with frustration. "If she hasn't been ill, why are you concerned about her?"

"She has been quite upset over not receiving any letters from her community."

"There weren't as many," Sister Alicia said sharply. "Because we were told by Sister Bridgett that Abigail was quite ill with pneumonia and unable to enjoy them in her weakened condition."

"We do have a Sister *Anita* who is suffering from pneumonia, and we do have a Sister Brianna who would have made that call. I wonder if your community was notified by mistake. I will look into it right away."

"Please do," she said as they approached room 142. Stepping ahead of Sister Janice, she walked into the room. "Abigail!"

"Alicia? Is that you, child?"

She rushed over to the nun's chair. "I'm here. Are you all right?"

Abigail placed her hands on Alicia's shoulders and began to weep.

"It's all right now—I'm here," Alicia soothed. "It's all right." She looked over at Sister Janice. "Would you leave us alone?"

"I thought I would take you over to the convent and get you settled."

Alicia took a deep breath. "Leave us—now."

"I'll be waiting outside the door."

Alicia stroked Abigail's back as Sister Janice left the room. In a quiet voice she said, "I sense a corrupted spirit in that woman. She has resisted my seeing you with her every motion—I must call the airport at once and make arrangements for a flight out tomorrow. Cold weather was moving into the Boston area when I left early this morning; it might be a little rough on those delicate lungs of yours."

Abigail wiped her eyes. "If I can regain my composure, there is much I need to tell you."

Sister Janice lingered in the hallway outside the door. "We can't speak freely now," Alicia warned with a whisper. "I will come back later."

"We must take Clare with us," Abigail said.

"Who is Clare?"

"You will meet her when you return. She must come with us."

"I don't see how I can do that. I have the authority to discharge you, but I have no authority over Clare."

"She must come."

"We will talk more later. Are you sure you are all right?"

"Despite my tearful display, I am well."

"I'm going to go over to the convent and get settled, then I will come back."

"You are staying at the convent?" Abigail asked.

"Sister Janice insisted."

Abigail gripped Alicia's arm firmly. "Hear me, Alicia. You must be careful. I think Sister Janice is under the influence of Sister Theresa, the same Sister Theresa who turned to the powers of darkness nearly a lifetime ago."

"The Sister Theresa who was made to leave The Order?"

"Yes."

"Are you saying Sister Theresa is here at Tranquil Garden?"

"Her influence is here. I suspect *she* is here as well."

"I believe you."

"Be on your way," said Abigail as she embraced the woman. "But be aware and be cautious."

Alicia lowered her head and waited. Abigail raised her trembling hand and made the sign of the cross on Alicia's forehead, as a whispered blessing passed through her lips. The younger nun straightened up and headed out the door.

She followed Sister Janice back to the main entrance and into the cream-colored van, where Robert sat in the driver's seat reading an article from a newsmagazine.

"We are ready to go to the convent, Robert," Sister Janice said.

He started the engine. "Will you want me to wait to take you back, Sister Janice? or should I go for the day?"

"You go on. I will walk back."

"We will walk back," Alicia added.

"Aren't you going to rest after your flight?"

Robert turned out of the driveway. "If it's just a matter of dropping off a suitcase, why don't I wait around and give you both a ride back?"

"No, no, no," insisted Sister Janice. "It will take a few minutes to show her around and get her settled. I imagine after the long trip this morning, she will reconsider and rest for a little while. You can just drop us off." She looked at Alicia in the back seat. "It's not far, less than a fifteen-minute walk."

"That will be fine."

Robert put on his signal less than a mile down the road, then he turned into another long driveway. "Here we are, Sisters."

"Thank you, Robert," Sister Janice said in a loving tone. "We appreciate you so much."

He shut off the engine. "I'll get the suitcase."

Alicia climbed out of the van and looked at the two-story building constructed in the same Spanish Colonial architectural style as the nursing home. She took her small suitcase from Robert.

"Let me know when you're going back to the airport, Sister, and I'll be happy to drive you. Mornings are best."

"I appreciate that. I will let you know."

"This way, Sister Alicia," Sister Janice said, taking a set of keys from her pocket and unlocking the door. "Sister Judith?" she called loudly. "Sister Judith?"

A young woman came into the entry. "Yes, Sister Janice."

"I want you to meet our guest, Sister Alicia."

"Just *Alicia* is fine," she interjected.

"Welcome, Alicia," Sister Judith greeted.

Sister Janice placed her hand on Sister Judith's shoulder and ushered her toward the door. "Would you please go over to Tranquil Garden and attend to my desk in my absence?"

"But I was told to stay here and show Alicia the guest quarters."

"I will take care of that," she said gently. "We will only be a few minutes."

Sister Judith opened the front door. "I will see you both later."

Sister Janice looked around the room. "Mother Francesca left a spare key to the front door yesterday, but where?"

"Is this it?" asked Alicia as she pointed to a key on the top of a telephone table.

Sister Janice compared it to her own. "This is the one. Keep it with you during your stay, then give it to one of the Sisters before you leave for the airport. It's empty around here now because everyone is working at Tranquil Garden, but by dinner this house will seem pretty crowded. When do you think you will be leaving?"

"I don't know yet, why?"

"Oh, no reason." She turned and pushed on a swinging door. "In here are the dining room and the kitchen. These tables are more than eighty years old. I don't think you can buy wooden tables that are this length any longer."

"They are beautiful."

"These four tables seat the twenty-nine Sisters of Mercy who live in this convent. We have other communities throughout the Southwest. It is fortunate that you are here when our Mother Francesca is here. She travels quite a bit keeping up with everything." Sister Janice began walking again. "Through these doors is the library, which has over two thousand volumes. Then down this hallway are the guest quarters. This way."

Alicia followed Sister Janice into a large suite. "Is there a phone in the room?"

"No, but there is one in the sitting room. You will be our only guest, so select any bed you want. The room was designed to hold four, but we have been known to squeeze in a few extra

whenever there is a special occasion. We had
seven sisters with us when one of our residents
celebrated her eighty-fifth jubilee. Can you
imagine being one hundred and two years old?"

Alicia walked over to a four-drawer
dresser. "May I use these drawers?"

"Help yourself." Sister Janice pointed to a
closed door on the other side of the room. "That
door leads to a full bath. There are fresh towels
and soap."

"Thank you, I would like to freshen up."

"Are you the youngest of your community?"

Alicia shook her head.

"I am the youngest one here. I thought you
might be the youngest, too." She pointed toward the ceiling. "The Sisters' rooms are located upstairs, and we ask that you not go up
there. You are welcome to go anywhere on this
floor—well, except for Mother Francesca's office."

"Where is that?" Alicia asked. "I don't
want to wander in there by mistake."

"Oh, you can't. You can only get to her office through the library, but it is never un-
locked, and only other Sisters of Mercy have the
key. Many of the valuable papers about the history of our community, and about the Sisters
who have been a part of it, are kept inside, along
with a small collection of rare books. Several
years ago, before I came, vandals damaged a

number of early photographs of this very convent being built. They also ruined several books, so Mother Francesca's office has been kept under lock and key ever since. Luckily, our most prized book wasn't damaged—our registry. It is a very old book. With a fine red leather cover and gold embossing. And inside this book there is an entry for every Sister of Mercy who has ever been professed. I've seen my name inside this book."

Alicia opened her suitcase. "What an honor for you."

"Mother Francesca wrote out my entry with a pen that had to be dipped in a bottle of ink. I have never seen such a thing. I always wrote with a pen that had the ink inside." She drew her hands up to her chest. "The sheer history of it is overwhelming. I must show it to you sometime before you leave."

Trying not to sound as disinterested as she was, Alicia said, "I will look forward to it."

Twenty-Eight

Leaving the Divine Mercy convent, Alicia walked toward Tranquil Garden. Though she wasn't aware of it, her fists were clenched tight. Her eyes revealed the urgency that consumed her thoughts. A passing car sent a cloud of dust up from the road. She watched the car take the east fork leading into the next town and drive out of sight.

When she turned her head toward the domed roof of the Tranquil Garden sanctuary, she saw the cross rising above it. The sight brought a sense of assurance, a reminder of hope.

In search of Abigail, Alicia made her way through the building toward room 142. Abigail was standing at the door.

"Have you been waiting out here the entire time I've been gone?"

"It wasn't so long. You made very good time. Clare is here. I must ask you to close the door, as I want our discussion to be as private as possible."

"Let me get you seated first."

Clare got up. "And I'll get the door."

Abigail leaned heavily on Alicia. "There is much to discuss." She situated herself in her chair and waited a moment. "Clare? Are you with us?"

"I'm beside Alicia."

"Let us take a moment for formal introductions. Clare, this is Alicia. Alicia, this is Clare."

"It's a privilege to meet you," Clare said.

"The man who drove me here from the airport, he told me you were very helpful to Abigail—thank you for all that you have done."

"Alicia," Abigail said, "do you recall the vision given to The Order following the removal of Sister Theresa?"

"Yes," she answered. "And they believed that Sister Catherine represented the old, withered leaf—but that could not have been the correct interpretation, since she died without The Order being restored."

Abigail adjusted her glasses. "I was given a vision very similar to that one. The vision came as I stood on the shore not far from here. In this vision, I saw an old withered leaf lying on a covering of white sand. Young and gentle hands picked up the leaf. Then, after a little while, it broke apart as if it had been crushed by some heavy object. The hands moved away, and there, lying on the sand, was another leaf even older and more withered than the first. I watched as this leaf transformed into a radiantly green leaf bursting with life. I continued to watch and saw eleven young green leaves appear. They encircled the one that had been old."

"Were you given an interpretation?" Alicia asked.

"I can not say this understanding was given to me by the Lord, but I believe that Sister Catherine represented the first old and withered leaf. The second is represented by the one who was to be of The Order, the one whose place Sister Theresa wrongly took."

"But there was no other," Sister Alicia argued. "The Lord brought no one else forward in all of the years that have passed since Sister Theresa."

"That is because He brought the one during the time of Sister Theresa, child—and that one sits with us at this very moment."

Alicia looked over at Clare. "You are the one?"

"She is," answered Abigail.

"But she isn't older than Sister Catherine by any means, and I wouldn't call her more withered either."

"It is my understanding," Abigail explained, "that the old appearance of the leaf represents wisdom, and the withered appearance represents humility. I can assure you that Clare surpasses Sister Catherine in each of these."

Alicia placed her finger to her lips as her forehead wrinkled in thought. "Shortly after Sister Catherine's death we began to receive applications from young women wishing to enter our community as postulants. We have accepted all of them except one. They will begin arriving at the end of this month to begin their six-month postulancy period before entering our novitiate class in October."

"How many postulants has the Lord brought to us?"

"Eleven," Alicia said.

"The exact number needed to restore The Order. The Lord has made His intentions clear. We must remove Clare from this place immediately," insisted Abigail. "Her life is in danger here. Remember the words to the final prophecy given by Sister Catherine."

> *"The innocent will perish in the fires set by trusted hands. But fear not, for out of these ashes will arise new life and greater glory for my name."*

"The innocent have already perished by trusted hands. Both of the nuns Clare arrived here with have died under peculiar circumstances. The first, Florence, took a fall down a flight of stairs. Then Gloria met a similar fate. Her body was discovered beneath the retaining wall. Clare will be next."

Alicia studied Abigail's face. "We should call the authorities."

"They will not listen to us. We must get Clare to safety first; then light can be shed on these dark deeds."

"Can we turn to anyone on the staff here?"

"I think it unlikely. And considering the ease with which Sister Janice seems to be made a willing accomplice, I would deal with her with great caution. She wove quite a snare of lies to keep us separated. I will assume you have not required surgery lately?" said Abigail.

"Is that why you thought I didn't come in January?" Abigail nodded in reply. "A woman by the name of Sister Bridgett, who sounded amazingly like Sister Janice, called me the day before my flight. She told me that you were ill, possibly with an infectious strain of pneumonia. She kept me well-informed about your condition, and promised to notify me as soon as it was safe to reschedule my visit. I spoke with her numerous times, but Sister Janice not only denied being the voice I heard on the phone, she informed me directly that there is no Sister Bridgett here."

"I was told of a snowstorm which hampered the mail. Then I was given a stack of letters written by Sister Janice herself." Abigail turned her head. "Clare, will you get the letters for Alicia?"

Clare went to the night table, opened the drawer, and retrieved the letters. "Here you are."

Alicia sorted through the letters. "But these *are* from us. They are unopened, but this is our stationery."

"They are unopened?" Abigail asked.

"All of them," Alicia answered. "These two are mine."

"Someone has taken the fraudulent letters with the Houston postmarks and replaced them with the letters that were being withheld from me. It seems they intend to question my mental capabilities."

"Then we won't mention them. I will just inform Mother Francesca that I intend to take you home a couple of weeks earlier than scheduled."

"And what about Clare?" Abigail asked.

"There are legalities involved. Taking her from Tranquil Garden might even be considered kidnapping."

"How can it be kidnapping?" Abigail protested. "She is coming of her own free will."

"But she has been admitted here. Papers have been signed."

Abigail's voice shook with emotion. "We can't leave her here."

"We won't, I promise you both that we won't. But I think it would be best to let it appear as if only Abigail and I are leaving. Maybe we can gain permission to have Clare accompany us to the airport to see you off."

"And if we can not gain permission?" Abigail asked.

"Then we'll just go and hope that we all don't wind up in a jail cell."

"When can you speak to Mother Francesca?"

"After dinner. That will give me time to arrange our flights out of Houston." Alicia looked at the clock on the wall. "I could do that now." She gave Abigail's hand a gentle squeeze. "If there are seats available, we will leave tomorrow."

"There must be seats available to some destination," said Abigail with certainty. "Do the best you can."

Alicia stood up. "I'll come back this evening after I've spoken to Mother Francesca and let you know when to be ready to leave."

After Alicia left, Abigail and Clare remained seated, offering silent intercessions until the hour arrived for dinner to be served.

"We should start making our way to the dining room," Clare said.

"Now that you mention it, I am feeling a bit hungry." Abigail got up with a muffled groan. "Shall we go and enjoy the delicious cheesy casserole our chefs have labored over on this particular Sunday?"

"They do have a way with noodles and cheese."

"As long as they do not attempt to conceal small bits of broccoli in the concoction as they did last week. That vegetable may prove to be the most valuable of them all, but it is one I have detested through the whole of my life. I would prefer to conclude that life without stumbling on the pungent source of fiber again."

Clare smiled. "I promise to let you know if I see any."

Twenty-Nine

Silverware clanked against china plates. Voices echoed off the white walls of the open room. The evening meal at the Sisters of Mercy convent was now under way.

"Would you like some mashed potatoes?" asked Sister Janice.

Alicia reached for the serving bowl. "Are those chives?"

"Yes, and they're fresh," Sister Angelica said. "That's Sister Pauline's trademark. Her potatoes are always loaded with them."

"Have you found your accommodations acceptable, Sister Alicia?" Mother Francesca asked.

"They are lovely, thank you."

"And have you had a chance to speak with Abigail?"

"Briefly."

"And Sister Alicia's visit has done wonders," Sister Janice said. She passed a bowl of steamed carrots to Alicia. "I went by to check on Abigail before coming over for dinner, and her spirits have never been higher."

"We have been quite concerned about her," Mother Francesca said as she picked up a knife from her place setting and began cutting a portion of chicken breast into bite-sized pieces. "I'm glad you were able to come so quickly and put her mind at ease."

"How long will you be staying with us?" Sister Angelica asked.

Alicia lowered her fork. "I spoke to the others from my community this afternoon about that, and we discussed bringing Abigail home early this year."

"I have also given that possibility some thought," Mother Francesca said. "Abigail is always welcome, but this year has been much more difficult for her than last year. Those who are younger more easily endure seasonal stays. We should review our policy on the matter." She reached for a tall glass of iced tea. "I am in complete agreement with you and your community, Alicia. Will you be discharging her?"

"Yes, I have already made flight arrangements."

Mother Francesca nodded. "And what day is your flight scheduled?"

"Soon. Tomorrow afternoon. I would like to have her at the airport by two o'clock."

Sister Janice pulled a small notebook and a pen from the pocket of her skirt, and flipped to a blank page, making a note of it. "I'll call Robert after dinner to arrange a ride to the airport."

"There is also some paperwork that will need to be completed," Mother Francesca said. "Can it be done in time?"

Sister Janice nodded. "I'll start on it this evening."

"Sister Abigail has kept us busy during her stay." Mother Francesca sprinkled salt over her carrots. "I will never forget the fierce look I received the last time I caught her using the unauthorized phone." She shook her head. "Mother Eltza might be in her nineties, but she is suffering from no loss of spark when it comes to getting what she wants."

Alicia's expression changed. Sister Janice looked at her. "Is something wrong?"

Alicia blinked her eyes several times as if just waking up. "Wrong? No—I—I just don't understand why Abigail wasn't allowed to place phone calls."

"The Sisters are supposed to make their calls through my desk for billing purposes," Sister Janice explained. "Abigail attempted a few phone calls from a phone in the dining room because she insisted that I wasn't placing the calls properly."

"But you were?" Alicia asked carefully.

"The problem was an incorrect number. I tried several times to explain what the problem was and to locate the correct number for her, but she insisted she had the right one, so day after day I dialed it for her."

Alicia forced a smile. "Abigail can be stubbornly insistent at times." Laughter swept briefly around the table. She had not noticed before how intently the other nuns sitting at the long rectangular table had been following the conversation. She looked at each of them, deciding that their presence could bring about the favorable response to the request she was about to present to Mother Francesca. "Abigail has grown rather fond of her roommate."

"We often see Clare helping Abigail negotiate the hallways," said Mother Francesca. "I am sure they will continue to correspond after Abigail's return to the Northeast."

"Would it be an inconvenience to have Clare accompany us on the drive to the airport?"

Mother Francesca looked up from her plate. The sounds of clicking forks and conversation continued throughout the room, but at their table every sound seemed to stop for a moment. Alicia held her breath as she realized she needed to look into the eyes of Mother Francesca. Though she displayed a confident expression, her heart began to pound. Alicia felt the presence of evil all around her. With the dread of looking upon a dead animal, horribly mangled by an encounter with a speeding car, Alicia slowly raised her gaze.

Mother Francesca's pale brown eyes waited with the same powerful dread. The two looked upon each other. A gripping sensation encompassed Alicia's heart. A prayer for those empty eyes struggled for release as indignation over the violent acts that had been orchestrated rose to overpowering proportions.

An intense wave of nausea swept over Alicia as she surrendered her desire for the divine desire stirring within her. Her lips parted, and in a hushed whisper that went unheard she said, "Jesus, have mercy on her soul."

Mother Francesca looked away. "I see no reason why Clare can not go. Do you, Sister Janice?"

Sister Janice swallowed a mouthful of food. "None at all. What a wonderful surprise for them. I will share the news first thing in the morning."

"I will be going over this evening," said Alicia as she pushed her plate away. "I would like to tell them."

Sister Angelica looked across the table at Alicia's nearly full plate. "Was there something wrong with your food?"

"I'm just not very hungry."

Sister Janice wiped her mouth. "Why don't I show Alicia the library?"

"I'm sure she will enjoy that," Mother Francesca said. "I will have Sister Angelica clear your places at the table." She motioned with her hand. "You go ahead and entertain our guest."

Alicia followed Sister Janice through the dining room. As they passed between two more of the long, rectangular tables, she noticed the other sisters were no longer carrying on conversations. She turned her head and looked back. The short hairs on her arms stiffened at the sight. They were all staring at her.

"We keep the door closed," Sister Janice said as they entered the library.

Alicia walked to the center of the large room. A portrait hanging above the fireplace drew her attention. She approached it slowly.

"Who is that?"

Sister Janice smiled. "That's Mother Francesca when she was young. It was painted shortly after her election as Superior General of the Sisters of Mercy. She was the youngest in our community's history to ever hold the office. Those were tragic days." She walked over to a portrait hanging on another wall. "This is our Mother Anne."

"She's beautiful."

"Mother Anne was killed by her nephew. It happened in Arizona before we established Tranquil Garden. They say her nephew was a sweet young man who showed possibilities of having a vocation himself. One afternoon, for no apparent reason at all, he strangled her."

"That's ghastly!" Alicia said.

"Yes, but God brings good from all things. Mother Francesca's years of service have blessed countless souls. Would you like to see the registry?"

"I would."

Sister Janice began walking toward a door at the back of the library. "I really enjoy historic things. I think I will ask Mother Francesca if I can chronicle the history of the Sisters of Mercy sometime." She reached into her pocket and retrieved a set of keys. "I wonder if anyone other than myself would be interested?"

"I'm sure the others in your community would."

"That's true." Sister Janice turned the key in the lock and opened the door. She reached for the light switch. "It's over here on a podium all its own."

"Could I see your name first?"

"I would be honored." She turned several pages of the open book. "There I am, first entry on the right-hand side."

"Your given name was Alice."

"That's almost *Alicia. Alice* is probably the American version, and *Alicia* is the European one. My professed name was actually Mother Anne's given name. On the left side are Sister Judith and Sister Angelica's entries. We were novices together." She turned back a few pages. "And here is Sister Josephine."

"Very nice. And where is Mother Francesca's name?"

"It's much further back." She turned more pages. "There it is, complete with the dates she received first Sacraments, the dates she took temporary and perpetual vows, and the date she was elected as Superior General." She pointed to the second column. "Did you see her baptismal name? What a sacrifice to give up such a breathtaking name."

Alicia could not remove her eyes from the name before her. There, in script, was written *Genevieve de Chantal*. Proof, beyond the growing suspicion, that Mother Francesca was indeed Sister Theresa. She realized with stark sobriety that Clare was in danger—a danger that was growing increasingly imminent.

Thirty

Thick clouds hid the moon. For the Sisters trying to find their way along the dark road, the lights coming from the windows of the Tranquil Garden Nursing Home served as beacons. They made their way slowly toward the lights, discussing the evening's plans. It took all of Alicia's strength to walk instead of run, to restrain herself, to act casual and unhurried.

"The paperwork won't take long," Sister Janice said. "I'll come get you when I'm finished. Probably around seven forty-five."

"I was planning to stay with Abigail until she retires for the night," Alicia responded.

"But you can't do that. Convent rules insist that our doors be closed by eight o'clock. And Mother Francesca doesn't allow for exceptions—and she won't let you walk back to the convent alone."

"I understand."

They walked quietly for a moment.

"I love the night," Sister Janice said. "Don't you?"

"I prefer the day."

"Everything is busy in the day. Ants. Birds. People. It's exhausting just thinking about all that rushing around. Night is stillness. I like that."

They turned and began walking down the driveway. An airplane flew overhead. Alicia looked at its blinking lights, wishing she were in there, along with Clare and Abigail.

"Why are you afraid?" Sister Janice asked.

"What makes you think I'm afraid?"

"I know things sometimes. Secret things. Sometimes I know what people like. Sister Abigail adores maple syrup, and she likes being outside. And sometimes I know why people are afraid. Sister Abigail is afraid something will happen to Sister Clare. So are you."

"Should we be afraid?"

Reaching Tranquil Garden, Sister Janice opened the front door. "Sister Clare will be lonely at first, but that is the price she must pay for enjoying such close friendship."

Alicia followed Sister Janice through the door and then hurried down the hall to room 142. She pulled the door free from the hardware that gripped its base to the wall and entered the room. "Abigail—I'm back, but I can't stay long. I have some things to tell you."

"You have managed to book passage on an airplane."

"For all of us."

"And you have arranged for Clare to accompany us to the airport as planned."

"Yes, she can come." The young woman sat down and took hold of Abigail's hands. "And I have something else to tell you, Abigail. I know which nun is Sister Theresa. While we were at the convent having dinner, Mother Francesca called you Mother *Eltza*. I knew it then; I looked into her eyes, beyond her eyes." Alicia shuddered. "I expected that you would not use that name outside our community. Later, when Sister Janice took me to see their community register, I asked to see Mother Francesca's record. When she pointed it out, I saw there, in front of me, the name: *Genevieve de Chantal.*"

Abigail rubbed her forehead as she absorbed the news. "I was not expecting this, children. I wish . . . I wish I could speak with her. If I thought she had ears to hear, I could offer her words to relieve her thirst for revenge."

"There is nothing you could say," Alicia said. "She has made her choice."

"But there is something she does not know. Something I pray the Lord will give me opportunity to say." Abigail patted Alicia's hand, then she said, "Is anyone else aware of your discovery?"

"I didn't say anything to anyone, but I had a strange conversation on the way over with Sister Janice. She told me she knows things—

secret things. She knew you and I were concerned about Clare."

"This is a counterfeit of the gift of the Word of Knowledge," Abigail said. "The one with this counterfeit is given limited insight into certain realms of spiritual knowledge. We must be cautious, even with our own thoughts, in her presence."

"When do we leave?" Clare asked.

"I've asked for a ride that leaves Tranquil Garden no later than one o'clock."

Abigail turned toward Clare. "That means we have some packing to do."

Alicia looked around. "It won't take us long."

"You have already labored enough for one day," Abigail said. "We will enjoy your company until it is time for you to leave, then Clare and I will pack our things."

Alicia noticed Clare massaging her temples. "Are you feeling well?"

Abigail answered, "She is suffering from her weekly cheese headache. Every Sunday we are served a cheesy casserole, and every Sunday evening she is stricken with a massive headache."

"Can I get you something?" Alicia asked with concern.

Clare put her hands down. "They bring me something a little later."

"Promptly at eight o'clock," said Abigail. "They bring the remedy. It is placed in a tiny cup on the night table where it sits until she is ready to retire for the evening. I have argued with her to no end to take it sooner, but she insists that if she does she will only awaken in the middle of the night with a throbbing head."

"If you're sure?"

"I am," responded Clare.

"Tomorrow night I will be back home!" said Abigail, her thoughts refocusing on the future. A wide smile parted her face. "I will be surrounded by so many long-time companions. I have sorely missed each of them. And when we get home, Clare, you will be happy to know that our kitchen only rarely serves any type of cheese at all."

Alicia looked at the clock on the wall. "It's going to be a long night. I'll be too worried about you both to sleep."

"There's no need to worry, child," Abigail comforted. "They will postpone whatever plans they had for Clare until after she returns from seeing us off to the airport. They have no idea that she will not be coming back."

Alicia sighed. "You're right."

"I hear a tapping sound," Abigail said. "Is someone at the door?"

"Good evening, Sisters," said Sister Janice as she walked in. "How are you feeling, Sister Clare?"

"Her Sunday headache has arrived right on schedule," Abigail answered.

"I was afraid of that," Sister Janice said. She raised her hands, revealing a large paper cup in one hand and a small, foil-sealed package containing two capsules in the other. "I picked these up from Nurse Louise on the way over. I thought you might like to have them a little early."

"That was kind of you," Clare said. "Just leave them on the night table."

"Don't you want to take them now?"

"I take them when I retire for the evening."

Sister Janice put the medication down. "We hear you are leaving us tomorrow, Sister Abigail. We will miss you."

"And I will miss your wonderful readings."

Sister Janice looked at Alicia. "We'd better start back. We don't want to be late. Sister Clare, will you be up to the trip to the airport tomorrow?"

"I'll be fine," Clare answered.

Abigail got up from her chair as soon as Sister Janice and Alicia left, and felt for the closet door. "There must be a knob here somewhere."

"Reach a little higher and to the left," Clare said.

Her old hands located the knob and opened the door. She lifted a suitcase from the floor and handed it to Clare. "That one is yours. Mine is on the shelf. I'll have to get a chair."

Clare put her suitcase on the bed. "No, you could fall. Let me try to reach it."

They packed their things and placed the suitcases inside the closet. Abigail washed and changed into her nightclothes, then Clare did the same. The final ritual of the night, the recitation of evening prayers, seemed to take longer than usual as both women struggled against the profound effects of the active day.

As Abigail lay down, exhausted, she tried to gather her thoughts and to focus on rest, on gaining strength for the day ahead.

Clare, instead, sat on her bed and opened her Bible. She managed a sizable reading before a searing headache began throbbing at her temples again. She took her weekly remedy, tore open the foil covers, and reached for the water cup. The capsules slid down easily. She smiled tenderly at Abigail, who was already in the light stages of sleep, pulled her feet into bed, and turned off the light.

She lay still, listening to the sounds of Abigail's breathing as the minutes slowly passed. Her eyes closed to welcome a restful sleep.

A silent call interrupted Clare's prayerful thoughts. Her eyes opened as she pulled off the covers and got out of bed. She approached Abigail's bed without fear, despite the increasing pain her movements brought.

"Who's there?" Abigail asked.

"Don't be afraid," Clare said softly. "It's me."

"And why are you seated on my bed, child?"

"I have a question to propose."

Abigail sat up. "And what question could you have at such an hour?"

"First, tell me the vision the Lord has blessed you with."

"Just as I was sleeping, I was shown a white rose in full bloom."

"Then here is the question. How many thorns have sprouted from the stem of this lovely flower?"

"What—what did you say?"

"I can only propose the question once."

Abigail cleared her throat. "The answer you seek is seven, one for each of the seven deadly sins that can pierce the soul of man. But why are you asking it of me?"

Clare laid her hands on Abigail. "Hear me, daughter. By the power of the Divine Name of Jesus Christ, receive the mantle of surrender to this, His holy will, and to the gentle yoke of servanthood to this, His Order."

"Yes, I do receive." She reached for Clare's hands. "What is happening, child?"

"I have completed all that the Lord has given me to do in the restoration of The Order."

"You are saying that He intends for *me* to complete this work of restoration?"

"I am."

"Surely this is a dream."

Clare fell forward into Abigail's embrace. "My death approaches."

"Let me get help."

"The poison has traveled too far."

Abigail moved out of the way and helped Clare lay down. "What do I do?"

"You sit."

"I am not up to the task," she answered. "Please say it isn't so."

"You desire to withhold heaven from me?"

"Never, child." As Abigail sat, she yielded to tears. She began to sob softly. "Oh, how I will miss you."

"Your days will be filled with the Lord's business as He—" Clare took a deep breath, "as He restores The Order through your hands. But the days will not be endless. We will meet again at the foot of the throne of the One we yearn to serve."

The sweet smell of myrrh filled the room. Abigail sat quietly as the breath of life left her friend.

Tomorrow would still bring the bright light of the new day and the physical limits imposed on her aging body, but it would also bring the promise of beginning.

Thirty-One

Tom glided his mop along the blue-bordered tiles of the southeast wing, being careful to leave a strip on the left for anyone who needed to get through. His movements were automatic after so many years, leaving his mind free for speculating. This morning he was speculating on the ominous good-bye his wife gave him when he left for work. "Death will come near you," she warned, "not once, but twice."

She had given these warnings before. Sometimes circumstances cooperated, sometimes they did not. He would have to wait and see.

"Good morning," Alicia said as she neared him. "Can I get through?"

"Just stay to the left, Sister."

She went inside room 142.

"Abigail?" There was no response. Alicia saw Clare lying beneath the covers of the old woman's bed. "Abigail?" she said again as she came toward Abigail, sitting in the chair near the bed.

"Clare is dead," she announced calmly.

"Her headache remedy was tampered with."
She displayed the package that housed the capsules. "In the center of the foil seal I felt a small hole. I believe a needle pierced this package. I further believe Clare was poisoned."

Alicia approached the bed. "That can't be." She examined the fingernails of Clare's left hand. They were the same blue hue as her lips. She stepped back from the body temporarily stunned. "I—I'll call the police."

"No," Abigail said strongly. "We must not raise questions until we have left this place."

"But she was murdered, Abigail."

"Yes, but The Order was not. She did not die before passing along the mantle of graces, child."

"In your vision you saw a second leaf, older, more withered." Alicia's eyes widened. "You received the mantle."

"And raising questions now about Clare's death will only bring chaos to this place. The authorities will surely question me, and that will put our travel plans, our safety, and The Order in jeopardy."

Alicia was silent for a moment as she considered the situation. She looked at Clare's body and then at Abigail. "Then, we'll say nothing until we are safely back at the Motherhouse."

"Good morning, Sisters," said Nurse Gertie

as she pushed her cart into the room. "Is Clare sleeping in this morning?"

"She's dead," Abigail said. "She went peacefully."

The nurse came closer and touched Clare's wrist and saw that there was no pulse. Working at Tranquil Garden, Nurse Gertie had seen many deaths. "Dying in your sleep," she said. "There's no better way."

"I think I should take Abigail to the dining room," Alicia said.

"I want to stay with Clare," Abigail said.

"We understand," Nurse Gertie said. "You can stay." She went out into the hallway for a few moments, then returned with Sister Janice.

The young woman looked at Clare. Her expression did not change. "Send for the removal team."

"Must we rush? Sister Abigail could use a little more time with her friend," said Nurse Gertie.

"And she will have that while we wait for the removal team."

"Yes, Sister."

Sister Janice turned toward Alicia. "It's frightening, isn't it, how you and Sister Abigail feared for Clare's life, and here she is, dead."

Janice left the room. Alicia moved to Abigail's side and held her hand. Minutes passed silently.

The sounds of flurried activity echoed in the hallway.

"Let's move out of the way," Alicia said.

"What is happening?"

"The staff is preparing to move the body."

"Be gentle with her," Abigail said as they came to the door. "They will be," said Alicia as she put her arm around the old woman. "We should head to the dining room. You haven't had breakfast."

"I couldn't possibly eat, not now."

"You must," Alicia said gently. "We have a long trip ahead of us."

"In view of that fact, and the fact that Clare seemed to cherish my thirst for maple syrup, I will try."

They both stood quietly until the gurney carrying Clare was rolled out of the room. Alicia helped the old woman down the tiled hallway. She noticed that residents were coming out of the dining room, not going in.

"I hope we aren't too late," Alicia said as they approached the buffet. She looked at the offerings. "There's not much left."

"A little late this morning, Sister Abigail," Robert said. "What can I get for you today?"

"I would like a bowl of oatmeal that is light on the butter with a full ladle of warmed maple syrup."

"You know I can't do that, Sister. How about some eggs?"

"But I must have it this morning of all mornings."

"I'm sorry, Sister, but you know . . ."

Alicia pounded the tray. "Get her what she wants."

Robert motioned to Sister Janice.

"Is there a problem?" she asked.

"Sister Abigail would like some oatmeal," Robert said.

"Then she should have it."

His face flushed with frustration. "But you said . . ."

"I said she should have it."

He prepared the bowl and passed it to Alicia. "Can I get something for you?"

"Nothing."

He nodded. "Sister Janice told me you need a ride to the airport. I'll be by to pick you up at one o'clock."

"We'll be ready." She placed the bowl on the tray. "Abigail, where do you want to sit?"

"I'm not ready for the company of others. Is there a vacant table?"

Alicia scanned the room. "Most of them are empty." She picked up the tray. "This way."

Abigail gripped Alicia's arm firmly. Her thoughts were not on the tragedy that had taken place the night before, but on the danger facing them at the moment, a danger that would not subside until they were finally off the grounds of the Tranquil Garden Nursing Home.

"Would you like coffee?" Alicia asked as she unloaded the tray.

"Only if you are having it."

"I'm jittery enough."

Alicia sat down and watched as Abigail savored her morning meal. She tried not to be concerned about Sister Janice, who stood less than twenty feet away looking in their direction, but as the minutes passed, it became impossible.

"Sister Janice hasn't taken her eyes off us since we got here."

"I would assume she is attempting to intimidate us as well as to use her counterfeit gift—those two always go together. She is surely seeking a dark access to the secret things of our hearts and minds. But she will be given only what she is allowed to be given. In the meantime, we must guard our hearts and minds, resting them entirely in Him."

"Given the circumstances, I find that hard to do."

"Don't give birth to any worries, child," Abigail said as she stirred her oatmeal. "His grace covers us like a blanket. She will gain no knowledge from us."

Thirty-Two

Graciella knocked on the open door of room 142. "May I come in, dear one?"

"I would appreciate the company. Sit with me."

"I have something for you." Graciella placed a soft, green leaf into Abigail's hand. "Your spirit is no longer old and withered and eager for death. You were the leaf beneath the one that was crushed."

Abigail touched the face of the leaf. "I am unworthy of the favor He has brought to me."

"We are all unworthy, dear one."

"Mercy sakes, Sister Abigail," Sister Kathleen said as she and Monica came into the room. "We just heard the news."

"Tell us it isn't true," Monica said.

"Let us go next door. There isn't room for all of us in here," said Abigail.

Sister Kathleen walked with the others to the workroom. "We sent word to Patrice. I'm sure she'll be along any minute. Should Sister Graciella be sitting in Clare's chair?"

"I have much to tell all of you once Patrice arrives."

"Here she is," Monica said.

"Is it true?" Patrice asked. "Where's Clare?"

Sister Kathleen looked over her glasses at Patrice. "Sit down so she can tell us what happened."

Abigail cleared her throat. "Let me begin by explaining a health malady Clare silently endured since her arrival. She suffered weekly from a severe headache brought on by eating cheese. Last night after eating a sizable portion of dinner, her torments began as usual."

"That chicken and rice casserole was loaded with cheddar cheese," Patrice said.

"It was colby," Sister Kathleen corrected.

"Whatever type of cheese it was," Abigail continued, "it produced the expected results. She took her remedy, which contained a fatal dose of medication or poison, and she died shortly thereafter."

"Clare was murdered?" Patrice asked fearfully.

"How could such a beastly act happen here?" Monica covered her eyes with her hands. "This is just horrible!"

"Clare—she knew she would be killed," Patrice said with unusual softness. "And she was so . . ."

"At peace," Sister Kathleen said. "I can't say I would have been."

"Your grief should be spoken, Sisters, but there is still great danger surrounding us." Abigail wiped the side of her tear-streaked cheek. "Before the murderous act took place, Sister Alicia was partaking of dinner at the convent of the Sisters of Mercy. Alicia made flight arrangements prior to the evening meal, but because she knew they would never allow Clare to leave Tranquil Garden, she devised a plan to secure permission for Clare to accompany us to the airport. No mention was made of Clare's boarding the plane with us." Abigail adjusted her glasses. "During that meal, Mother Francesca referred to me as *Mother Eltza.*"

"Mother Eltza?" Sister Kathleen asked with confusion. "This doesn't make any sense at all. What do flight arrangements have to do with you being called Mother Eltza?"

"That was the name Clare was going to tell us," Monica said.

"Yes. And, of course, hearing me referred to as *Mother Eltza* startled Alicia, as it's a name known only to those in my community. Her suspicions were confirmed when a tour of the library revealed Mother Francesca's Baptismal name—*Genevieve de Chantal.*"

"Precious Lord!" Monica said with alarm. "That was Sister Theresa's name."

"Indeed it was. Alicia came over after making the discovery," Abigail continued. "We continued discussing our travel plans. Despite this new revelation, it seemed that everything was arranged. In less than twenty-four hours, we three would arrive safely at the Motherhouse. I was feeling quite confident, too confident. Sunday after Sunday I heard Clare tear open the medicine package. It never occurred to me that someone would tamper with it."

"Maybe no one did," Monica said with new hope. "Maybe Clare died naturally."

"I agree. We've had enough stress around here to do even a healthy person in," said Sister Kathleen.

"I witnessed her death, and I can assure you it was not natural." Abigail held up the empty medicine package. "Here is the proof."

Patrice took the small plastic rectangle and examined it. "There's a little hole in the middle."

"That hole was made by a needle," Abigail said.

Sister Kathleen took the package from Patrice. "Looks like it. What do the police say about this?"

"They have no knowledge of this or of Clare's death—nor will they. My life depends on it."

No one spoke.

"Alicia," Abigail said with a sudden urgency. "She will be frantic if she doesn't find me in the room."

"I'll look for her," Patrice said. She walked to the door and looked out. "I think this is her coming up the hall now." She stepped out. "Alicia?"

The young woman quickened her pace. "Yes?"

"Abigail's in here."

Alicia came over to the long wooden table. "I notified Sister Mary Margaret that you are leaving today and gave her the address to the convent."

"Thank you, dear. Sit down with us."

"I don't want to interrupt."

"This is for you to hear. Sisters, let me introduce Alicia from the Sisters of the Divine Name Motherhouse."

"Have a seat," Monica invited.

"You talked about your plans—you are leaving us today, Sister Abigail?" asked Sister Kathleen.

"Yes, and very soon. There is much that must be done. Begin your prayers now, Sisters, for me, and for the task I have been given to complete. We have eleven postulants who must be prepared for the opening of the new novitiate class. I believe the Holy Spirit will train them and further prepare them for their places in The Order."

"But there is no Order," Patrice said strongly. "It's over."

"It is *not* over," Graciella said with conviction.

In unison, the nuns all turned toward Graciella.

"Before she died," Abigail explained, "Clare came to me. She laid hands on me and recited the words of the ancient prayer of consecration into The Order." Abigail opened her hand, revealing the leaf that Graciella had given her. "Clare was the leaf held in hands that appeared trusting and gentle. I was the older and more withered leaf beneath." She smiled. "As vain as I have been throughout my life it seems only just that my Lord portrays me as a withered leaf." She ran her fingertips along the face of the leaf. "I once mourned my life. My prayers were filled with pleadings for our Lord to have mercy on my tired spirit and bring about my death. He has transformed that spirit into one eager to labor. And there is much to be done, but the first step is to leave here safely."

"Abigail will be Mother Francesca's next target," Patrice said.

"At the moment I am sure Mother Francesca is unaware of the mantle of graces passing to me, and we must keep it that way. Say nothing about these events outside this room. But also be aware to guard your hearts and minds concerning the mantle passed on to me."

"We're dealing with a counterfeit gift," Alicia explained. "Sister Janice may be able to understand segments of secrets in the mind and heart. Used for good, her ability is the Gift of Knowledge. Used for evil, the corrupted gift brings destruction."

"I've never heard of such a thing," Sister Kathleen said. "And what does Sister Janice have to do with this?"

"Sister Janice has clearly joined forces with Mother Francesca." Alicia paused to look into the eyes of each Sister. "Abigail is in great danger."

Sister Kathleen said, "I wish we were all getting out of here."

"There is nothing to fear. The danger will leave with me." Abigail reached for Monica. "What time is it?"

"Eleven o'clock. They will be serving lunch shortly."

"And I feel the need for a warm bowl of soup. Shall we go together?"

Sister Kathleen got up from her chair. "I don't know if you should be eating anything, Sister Abigail. What if Mother Francesca has someone deposit a little poison into your broth?"

"Don't even think such a thing," Monica scolded.

"Abigail?" Alicia asked with concern.

In a tone of calm authority, Abigail responded, "Mother Francesca suspects nothing. She believes the victory is won. You have nothing to fear." Abigail moved her chair back and stood up slowly. "Who will join me in a nice warm bowl of soup?"

"I—I shouldn't," Monica said with hesitation. "I will only give you away."

"She does have one of those faces that doesn't hide things well," said Sister Kathleen. "Always has."

Abigail reached for Monica's hand. "Our Lord has made you stronger than you know." She pushed herself up from the table. "Now, would anyone else care to join Monica and myself?"

"We all will," Sister Kathleen said.

The trip to the dining room seemed to take longer than ever before, as the weariness of the sleepless night made Abigail's every step a challenge.

"I'll find you a wheelchair," Alicia said.

"Please," Abigail whispered. "Stay near."

"What is it?"

"Mother Francesca and Sister Janice are nearby."

"Are you sure? I don't see anyone."

"I'm sure. Meeting them now will prove to be a great strain for Monica."

"Yes, I noticed she was very fearful. She could put us all in danger." Alicia turned around and caught a glance of the shaken nun. "Should we turn around?" she asked Abigail.

"It's too late, child."

Turning the corner, Mother Francesca and Sister Janice approached the group of nuns and stopped them.

"Where are you going?" Sister Janice asked.

Alicia answered, "Into the dining room."

Sister Janice stepped in front of Monica. "You are too early. Lunch is served at eleven-thirty. Go back to your rooms."

"We have already come this far," Alicia said calmly. "Could we wait in the dining room?"

"Shall we accommodate their request?" Mother Francesca asked.

Sister Janice looked at Monica. "Is something wrong?"

Sister Kathleen took a step forward. "We all loved Sister Clare, Monica especially. Well—frankly, she is wearing us out with her tears. If you turn us back now, she might fall so far into her sadness that even a slice of chocolate pie won't snap her out of it."

"But she doesn't like chocolate pie." Sister Janice placed her hand beneath Monica's lowered chin and raised Monica's head until their eyes met. "Do you?"

"No."

Sister Janice continued looking at Monica. "Are you going to be all right?"

"By His strength—yes."

Sister Janice looked away from the loving eyes, and she moved her hand away from Monica's chin with a sudden quickness. "Continue on your way, Sisters."

Thirty-Three

A morning rain had left the ground wet and the sky gray.

"Our ride to the airport should be here by now," said Alicia as she looked out the window. "Where is he?"

"Robert is a dependable young man," Abigail said. "He will come."

"I want us safely on our way. Now, before we come across Mother Francesca again."

"No, I will meet her one final time. She will make one final choice."

Alicia turned toward Abigail. "Are you telling me you *intend* to see Mother Francesca before we leave?"

"And I intend to see her alone."

"No, Abigail," said Alicia with alarm. "We shouldn't risk such a meeting."

"The Lord is aware of the dangers, child. Take comfort in knowing this encounter is His will."

After a moment's pause, the younger woman left, and Abigail sat alone. For some time she listened to the silence with closed eyes. The spiritual battle was upon her, but it would not come before she received the divine strength she sought. The sound of footsteps coming up the hallway signaled the arrival and brought her prayer to an end. Abigail's eyes opened to the blurred figure of Mother Francesca standing before her.

"I know who you are," Abigail said.

"Then I am disappointed. I was looking forward to surprising you." Mother Francesca smiled. "And I know who you are, Mother Eltza. It was a long wait for victory, but it is one that is entirely mine." She took hold of a wheelchair parked beside the wall and pushed it over toward Abigail. "The pleasure of completing my task was beyond expression. The Order is no more, which means the Sisters of the Divine Name will be no more. How I will look back and relish this day."

"There will be consequences to the works you have wrought—consequences of eternal significance."

Mother Francesca leaned over and placed her face within inches of Abigail's. "Should I shiver now? Tell me what terrible punishment your Lord has in store for me that could hamper this victory?"

In a firm voice Abigail answered, "He will leave you as you have chosen to be—alone and blind."

"What a foolish answer. I am neither alone nor blind. I am surrounded by those who cherish me, and I see clearly enough to know that your Lord was powerless against me. For fifty-four years I labored and waited, expecting a strenuous battle. My victory was perversely easy. Your Lord did nothing to hinder my crushing the last remnant of The Order. He offered no help as the only one who could pass along the mantle of such detestable graces was breathing her last."

"It appears as you say."

She stood up straight. "Remind your community that they serve a powerless Lord, Mother Eltza."

"I will remind them of His compassion and mercy."

"Where was His compassion and mercy when my parents pleaded for their lives? When I was made to endure the advances of Colonel Schmidt? When my brothers collapsed from constant labor and sparse rations? Where was His mercy and compassion when the Sister of the Divine Name closed the door in our faces, sentencing my family to death?"

"There is more to the story."

"Is there?" she asked without interest.

"A vision was received by one of The Order only weeks before your family arrived at our convent in Belgium. The vision prophesied that the Sisters in Belgium would themselves be-

come the victims of the Nazis. They didn't
know exactly when, but they knew it was imminent. The Sisters put all their energies into securing sanctuary for those they had been
sheltering. It was impossible for them to take in
any others."

"That's a lie."

"The Sister who refused your family sent
me a letter about the grief it caused her. It was
the last letter she ever wrote. Only days after
your family was turned away, the Nazis came to
the convent door. They led everyone to a field
behind the convent. Each one was shot and
killed. Had your family been inside the convent,
all of you would have been executed as well. By
closing that door to your family, God was saving
your life."

"More lies. I've heard you are quite the
storyteller. But I am not interested in your stories."

"It is the truth."

"It isn't. And I will hear no more. The victory is mine. The Order is no more."

"But it is," Abigail said softly. "It continues through me."

The muscles in Mother Francesca's face
tightened. She walked around to the back of the
wheelchair. "Get in."

Abigail did as she was told. She felt the
wheelchair beginning to move.

"Where are we going?"

Mother Francesca did not answer. She pushed the wheelchair toward the rear exit, walking quickly despite her advanced years.

"Turn from the evil that consumes you before it is too late," pleaded Abigail.

They came outside, the wheels of the chair squeaking as they rolled over the rain-wet ground. She spoke again, this time with more intensity. "Don't let the choice that destroyed your life also destroy your eternity."

"My eternity?" Turning the chair toward the retaining wall, Mother Francesca said, "Hell can be no worse than living with the horrors I saw and endured." The wheelchair rocked and swayed as the terrain grew more treacherous. "How does it feel knowing you are about to die?"

"I fear nothing."

Breathing hard, Mother Francesca stopped the wheelchair. In front of them, inches away, was a thirty-foot drop, more than enough to ensure that Abigail would not recover. Mother Francesca looked at the rocks and hard sand, at the litter and debris that had been washed up by the tide. She was satisfied.

The rain from that morning had created puddles in the sandy mud covering the drop-off. The sun's light peeked through a momentary gap in the clouds.

Abigail said, "I hear the ocean."

Mother Francesca shielded her eyes

against the sudden brightness of the sun. "Get up."

"I assume we are near the edge of the retaining wall, and I assume you would have me stand from this chair amidst the mud, lose my balance, and find myself broken to pieces as Gloria did."

"Get up."

"I will not."

"You will."

"This evil deed you will have to do yourself. I will not do it for you."

"As you wish."

Mother Francesca pushed hard on the handgrips, but the chair did not advance. She pushed again, yet its position did not change. Abigail folded her hands in her lap as Mother Francesca continued to strain. She moved around to the front of the chair and tried to wrestle the hand brakes loose.

Abigail felt the chair jerk to one side as a frustrated moan left her attacker.

"Don't do this," Abigail said.

Mother Francesca grabbed Abigail's arm and pulled with enough force to raise her slightly in the seat. "Out of the chair."

"I will make no effort to bring about my death."

She pulled again. "Get up."

"He was saving your life, Genevieve. . . . He was."

"I had no life." Her foot slipped in the mud. "I had only pain and hatred and nightmares."

Wincing against the pain of another pull, Abigail said, "It was not the life He intended for you. His desire was for you to know joy and happiness, love and compassion."

"More lies," she shouted. "He took away all those things when He stripped me of my family."

"The Lord did not do that horrid thing."

"He did," she said with coldness.

"He did not abandon you, Genevieve."

Mother Francesca let go of Abigail and took a step back as if the old woman's words had knocked her off balance. She looked at the old woman, then at Tom, who was quickly approaching. She lunged forward, gripping both of the old woman's arms in her desperate hands.

Abigail felt the force of the pull as the sound of sloshing mud beneath someone's feet grew louder. She looked quickly from left to right. The blurred figures in front of her were locked in a fierce battle.

She heard a man grunt, followed by more sounds of sloshing mud.

Then, silence.

Abigail listened to the sounds of hard breathing for a moment.

"Who's there?"

"It's me, Sister—it's Tom."

"Tom. What happened?"

He looked over the retaining wall at the figure below and grimaced. "She's not moving." He fought to catch his breath. "I think she's dead."

"She was going to push me."

"I saw that." He coughed and cleared his throat. "I was watching from the window. Looked like she was taking you for a walk at first." Tom easily released the hand brakes on both sides of the wheelchair. "Lucky thing you set those brakes."

"I didn't set them."

"Those brakes were set solid, Sister." He pulled the wheelchair away from the retaining wall. "Must have been angels or something."

"Indeed."

As he began pushing the wheelchair, Tom said, "Let's get you inside."

"I must ask a favor."

"Anything, Sister."

"Say nothing about what you saw between myself and Mother Francesca. My life is in danger as long as I remain at Tranquil Garden. The circumstances of her death will only interfere with my departure. My ride to the airport is waiting by the front entrance. Please, allow me safe passage."

"Then I better take you around front."

The bumpy ride became smooth once they reached the sidewalk. A welcome warmth went through her body as the afternoon breeze brushed against her. A blur she reasoned to be the nursing home van came into view when they turned the corner.

"Abigail," Alicia said with alarm. She hurried over. "There's mud on your clothes. What happened?"

"Draw no suspicion toward me, child. We must be on our way while our passage is still allowed."

Tom rolled the wheelchair over to the side of an idling passenger van.

"What is everyone doing over here?" Sister Janice asked. "Abigail was supposed to be in her room until I brought the discharge papers."

"We went on one last ground tour," Tom said.

Reaching for the discharge papers, Alicia said, "I will take those."

"Let's get you up in the van, Sister," said Tom.

"How are we going to do that?" asked Alicia.

Sister Janice pointed to Tom. "Why don't you take her left side while Alicia and I take her right side."

"That will not be necessary," Abigail said.

Alicia brushed her bangs off her forehead

with the palm of her hand. "That won't work. Someone needs to be behind her in case she falls."

"Tom should get in the back," said Sister Janice.

"I am not an invalid," Abigail said loudly. She got up from the wheelchair. "And this is not some steep mountainside. I will manage."

Tom helped Abigail into the van.

"Tom, your shoes are covered in mud," Sister Janice said.

He closed the door behind Abigail and waved to Robert. "There's been an accident. You better come with me."

"They sure headed off quick," Robert said, as he watched Sister Janice and Tom head for the retaining wall. "Sister Janice didn't get a chance to say good-bye. Do you want me to wait until she gets back?"

"That won't be necessary, young man; do proceed," said Abigail.

"What accident was that man talking about?" Alicia asked as she buckled Abigail's safety belt.

"The meeting Our Lord arranged for Mother Francesca had a disastrous conclusion."

"What happened?"

"She attempted to send me over the retaining wall."

"Abigail," Alicia said with a gasp. "She didn't!"

"But my death was not supposed to be." She tugged at her safety belt. "Instead, she was the one who perished this day."

"Strengthen us, Lord! You mean she died?"

"She fell without so much as a cry, but it was not before the truth was spoken to her."

Alicia looked out the back window as they pulled away from the Tranquil Garden Nursing Home. She reached for Abigail's hand and held it tightly. The events of recent days still left a feeling of uncertainty within her. "Is it over?"

"The powers of darkness never tire of starting their wars. We have won this battle, but there will be others." A tired smile parted her face. "What better way does Our Lord have to keep us spiritually alert?"